Brooks

CHRIS
KENISTON

Indie House Publishing

Indie House Publishing

BOOKS BY CHRIS KENISTON

Aloha Series
Aloha Texas
Almost Paradise
Mai Tai Marriage
Dive Into You
Shell Game
Look of Love
Love by Design
Love Walks In
Waikiki Wedding

Surf's Up Flirts
(Aloha Series Companions)
Shall We Dance
Love on Tap
Head Over Heels
Perfect Match
Just One Kiss
It Had to Be You

Honeymoon Series
Honeymoon for One
Honeymoon for Three

Family Secrets Novels
Champagne Sisterhood
The Homecoming
Hope's Corner

Farraday Country

Adam

Brooks

Connor

Declan

Ethan

Finn

Grace

ACKNOWLEDGEMENTS

There is no way any of my books could be written without an enormous amount of support and contribution from friends and family.

Top of the list for *Brooks* has to be friend and author Kathy Ivan for letting me invade her home every afternoon to keep me honest. And of course Mary Sullivan for loving all things craft and cooking and—cake. I also need to shout out to military SEALs author Dale Mayer for putting up with me on the Florida shores and teaching me about olive oil and brain fog.

The aha moment of brilliance for this hero goes to Elizabeth Essex. Historical author extraordinaire, she's also pretty dang good with killer last lines!

Thank you all !

CHAPTER ONE

Brooks Farraday stripped off his surgical gloves and flung them across the room. He'd done everything he could to stabilize the eighty-year-old woman, but Sam had waited too long to bring Liza in. With the closest major medical facility capable of doing emergency heart surgery more than an hour away, there wasn't a damn thing more Brooks could do. Frustration clawed at him as he crossed the room, picked the gloves off the floor, and slammed them into the bin. Damn, he hated days like this.

The last thing he wanted was to face Sam. Only last week the whole town had turned out for their sixtieth wedding anniversary. Brooks' storefront set up here was small: a waiting room, a converted kitchen for a lab, an oversized closet that passed for his office, and two exam rooms. The corridors of the Taj Mahal wouldn't have been long enough of a walk to forestall the inevitable. Huddled before him, Sam and the handful of his and Liza's eight children and their spouses who still lived in or near town stared up at Brooks. No matter how hard he tried through the years to avoid expression of any emotion, the loss had to have shown. Two of the daughters burst into tears.

"I'm so sorry," he said.

Gray-haired and of wiry build, Sam ducked his chin, "You done all you could. I know that. Me and Liza thank you for that much." The old man turned and walked out the door before Brooks could offer to let him say his last goodbyes.

"We knew this day was coming, Brooks. Mom's heart has been threatening her for almost a decade." Sam and Liza's oldest son gave Brooks a pat on the arm, shifted his gaze across the small room, and then turned away. "I'd better catch up with Dad."

In a whirlwind of motion, the remaining siblings offered some words before chasing after their father.

Nora Brown, his RN, came up behind him. "I've called Andy at the funeral home. He's on his way over."

Brooks bowed his head. He was supposed to save lives.

"Also, Meg called, wanted to remind you about her friend. She suggested tonight would be a good night to join them for supper."

Letting his eyes fall shut, he blew out a tired breath. He was not up to socializing.

"She also said to tell you Friday night would be good too if you prefer."

His future sister-in-law seemed able to read his mind from across town even before he knew what he was thinking. Heaven help his brother Adam. Anticipating the arrival of her college friend for the wedding, Meg had been bouncing around for days like a little girl with a new jump rope. But then, yesterday she'd called him worried about her friend's odd behavior and asked Brooks to stop by for dinner to see if he noticed it too. He nodded at Nora waiting patiently for a response. "Thanks. I'll give her a—"

The front door burst open and Paul Brady came rushing through. "It's time, doc. Betty Sue, she's in the car. Says she ain't moving. Sent me to come get you."

Brooks turned on his heel, shouting over his shoulder, "How long has she been having contractions?"

"Don't know. But the pains are coming five minutes apart."

Trotting toward the car tilting awkwardly with one wheel on the curb, Brooks almost smiled at the crazed parking job. *First-time parents.*

The expectant father beat him to the vehicle, yanking the passenger door open.

"Hey, Doc," Betty Sue said through clenched teeth.

"How's it going? Think we can get you inside?"

Betty Sue panted through a contraction, nodding her head,

and then let out a long deep breath. "What I really want is to push, but if you'll give me a hand." She stuck out her arm and leaned forward. "With Ricky Ricardo here helping, I wasn't sure we'd make it."

This time, Brooks did chuckle at the *I Love Lucy* reference. He had no trouble envisioning Paul Brady scattering about like Ricky Ricardo had when his TV son was born. "At least he didn't leave you behind," Brooks said through a lazy smile as he eased his arm around Betty Sue and hefted her onto her feet. Only then did he catch the glare she shot her husband's way. "He didn't?"

"He did. Halfway to the road before he turned around to get me." Betty Sue made it as far as the threshold before doubling over with another contraction.

"Breathe," Brooks encouraged. By his estimation, her contractions were only two or three minutes apart. If they didn't hurry up and get her settled in, he might very well be delivering this baby on the sidewalk. "How long have you been in labor?"

The very pregnant woman blew out another deep breath. "Woke up around five this morning with some of those Braxton Hicks contractions, but by around seven I realized they were real labor pains. Not too close. Prepared myself for a long day." She moved forward into the waiting room. "But about an hour ago they started coming really fast."

"Well, it looks like, for a first baby, Paul Junior is in a hurry."

Andy from the funeral home came through the open door and stopped short. He had the good sense to wait until Brooks and his patient were past the first exam room before looking to Nora for answers.

"Room one," was all Nora said.

In the second exam room, Brooks and Paul settled Betty Sue onto the bed. Slightly larger than exam room one with a nice bed and some homey decorations nearby, this space doubled as a birthing room. Behind them, Nora came in and set up the oxygen. Just in case.

"Let me take a look." As Brooks had expected, Betty Sue was

fully dilated and effaced. Baby Paul was ready to make his entrance. "I know you want to push, but I need a few more seconds here."

Panting through another contraction, Betty Sue nodded and stretched her hand out for her husband. In what proved to be a routine, though speedy, delivery, in only fifteen minutes, Paul Brady Junior slid into the world.

"You ready to hold your son?" Brooks asked Betty Sue.

With a smile brighter than a kid's on Christmas morning, the new mother stretched out her arms. Paul kissed his wife's forehead and then did the same to the top of the tiny boy's head.

"We'll have to weigh him and do a couple of standard tests, but that can wait a few minutes for you three to get acquainted." Brooks stepped back, his gaze on the newborn infant. Brooks' heart was lighter. The circle of life. "Welcome to the world, young man. Welcome to the world."

• • •

"I'll see your five and raise you five." Antoinette Castelano Bennett tossed a couple of chips into the growing pile. When she'd envisioned coming to west Texas to visit her college roommate before her wedding, playing poker with the geriatric crowd wasn't exactly the pastime she'd pictured.

"I'm out." Dorothy Wilson, a sweet and friendly older lady, set her cards face down on the table.

"Me too." Sally May, an attractive woman with salt and pepper hair in a simple French twist and a German shepherd curled up at her feet, set her cards down with a sigh.

"Guess that leaves me." Eileen Callahan, the matriarch of the family Toni's friend was marrying into, had a grin as wide as the west Texas horizon. Adding more chips to the pot with one hand, she laid her five cards out, face up, with the other. "Three aces."

The last member of the group, Ruth Ann, let out a frustrated groan. A short, very thin woman with long, gray hair clipped in a sloppy pony tail, wearing jeans and a blue long sleeve shirt, she reminded Toni of everything she would have pictured a rancher's wife to be. Except instead of talking about cattle or chickens, every other sentence had something to do with her recent bunion surgery. "That leaves me out. Got two pair, king high."

This left only Toni holding cards. Remembering what her grandmother used to say, "Lucky in cards, unlucky in love," she wasn't feeling very triumphant. "Sorry ladies. Full house: three queens over a pair of tens."

"I'm going to take a walk to the ladies room." Sally May pushed to her feet. "Maybe it will change my luck."

Next to deal, Eileen gathered the cards from the table. "So tell us more about this traveling husband of yours?"

Separating the winning till into appropriate colored stacks, Toni considered what to say. The call that had sent her husband packing his bag and rushing to Logan Airport for a flight to one of those -*stan* countries had been an unexpected gift. William never did off-shore sites anymore, but when the engineer assigned to this project suffered a massive heart attack on his way to the airport, the partners scrambled for a replacement project manager, and William was the only person with enough flexibility and skill to go.

Remembering the harrowing twenty-minute rush had her gripping her chips more tightly.

"Damn it, Antoinette. There's too much starch in my shirts. Again."

"I'm sorry." She hated ironing shirts. "Maybe this one will be—"

William snatched the shirt out of her hand and slammed it into his suitcase. "I don't want to wear that shirt on the plane."

Toni bounced back from his reach. She wasn't making that mistake again.

"If that dumb knot-head at the dry cleaners can get the starch right there's no reason you can't. You don't have to be a Rhodes Scholar to iron a shirt."

"Toni?" Eileen's hands had stilled mid-shuffle, her brows pinched with concern.

"Sorry, my mind wandered. Yes. William doesn't travel much anymore. He's very protective of me. Doesn't like to be away from me at all, but he didn't have any choice this time."

"Well, it was very fortuitous that his extended trip coincided with my wedding, even if I had to use my best debate skills to get you to come visit now instead of only for the wedding weekend." Meg O'Brien—soon to be Farraday—stood at Toni's side, a coffeepot in hand. "Sounds like he turned out to be a very loving husband."

"Yes. Loving." Under the table, Toni clenched her hands together, forced the plastic I'm-so-happily-married smile she always used in public, and pushed aside her husband's last words on his way out the door.

"I don't know how reliable the satellites are in that God-forsaken temporary engineering camp. For God's sake don't forget to charge your phone. Better yet, stay close to home. In that armpit of a country, who knows what I might need ..."

She knew what close to home meant. Not that it would be hard to do. Where did she have to go?

"My mother will be back from her cruise in a few weeks. When she returns, I'll arrange for you to stay with her while I'm gone." His gaze darted about the pristine condo. "I'll be back much sooner than three months if I have anything to say about it. That mud-hole corner of the world is no place for a man like me."

She nodded. Not sure what he expected her to do next. Would this be the time he'd want her to hand him the rest of his things to make packing go faster, or would this be when nothing she did would be right? The outburst over the shirt had her thinking she'd be better off waiting for instructions. Maybe.

"Meg is right." Eileen dealt the cards. "It's always nice to have friends visit. And she tells me you're quite the cook too? She needs some fattening up. Working here every morning and fixing up that old house the rest of the time, she's wearing herself to a skeleton. Which reminds me," sorting her hand, Eileen looked over her shoulder at Meg, "I've almost got the drapes done for the old parlor. These are the last of the curtains."

"Sounds like time for a decorating party." Sally May picked up her cards.

Eileen nodded. "It's been fun bringing that old house back to life."

From what Meg had told Toni, the Farraday clan spent more time putting around the old Victorian than they had at their own homes, and Meg seemed to love every minute of suddenly being part of a large tight-knit family. Toni couldn't imagine. Whenever her husband's family descended on Boston, helpful wasn't the first word that came to mind.

"Sounds good." A customer across the café waved Meg down, and she took off in their direction.

When Toni married William and settled in the bustling heart of Boston's Back Bay she thought she'd won the lottery. Watching Meg smile and flutter from table to table, glowing from the inside out, Toni wondered if she'd ever been that happy. Barely glancing at her cards, Toni tossed the hand onto the table. "I think I'm going to sit this one out. Could use a little fresh air."

"Oh, good." Ruth Ann sprang up laughing. "I'll sit in the hot seat while she's gone."

Meg came hurrying back to the table. "You ready to go? I've got about another half hour till Shannon comes in."

"I was just going to stretch my legs, but maybe a nice walk home would be better."

Meg studied her a little longer than she'd have liked. "Good idea. Back door is unlocked. I'll get home as soon as I can."

"No hurry."

"Can you find your way?"

Toni almost laughed. The town wasn't that big, and what there was of it, had been built in a basic grid. It might take her all of fifteen minutes to walk down Main Street and then turn up onto Meg's block. "I'll be fine."

"Will we see you for Saturday's card game?" Dorothy Wilson looked up. "Nora comes on Saturdays."

"I don't know. Depends on how much work there is to be done at Meg's," Toni said.

"Work, my foot!" Meg winked at her friend. "Saturday we're heading to Abilene. I've got some more shopping to do."

"I'm in." Toni smiled at her friend and realized for the first time in a very long time she was doing an awful lot of heartfelt smiling.

Though she'd seen the Main Street shops driving through town before, she took her time now, glancing at the people coming and going, spending an extra minute or two looking at the window displays. The inside of the Cut and Curl looked like it hadn't changed much since the day it was built. In a line along the back wall were several of the old-fashioned massive hair dryers. Even now, two women sat side by side flipping through magazines.

When Toni pictured West Texas she had a vision of Clint Eastwood chasing cows down a dirt road flanked by wooden sidewalks. She hadn't pictured Mayberry.

About to turn the corner to Meg's street, a muffled woof caught her attention. Still too far from the residential part of the block for there to be a nearby yard with a dog, she paused and looked around. Nothing. A few more steps and she heard it again, only this time the sound had more of a whine to it. Where was it coming from?

Taking her time to scan the area, Toni inched slowly forward, listening carefully. There it was again, a little louder, and coming from across the street. Almost willing the animal to show itself, she stepped off the curb. Movement in the shrubs alongside a boarded up house told her she was heading in the right direction when a black muzzle appeared, followed by a furry body and at last a drooping tail…Walking in her direction…With a limp.

For a short second she'd thought it might have been Sally May's German shepherd but then realized this dog was more gray than tan and a bit shorter than the eighty-pound shepherd. "Oh, sweetie." Nearly to the other side of the street, she squatted down for the dog to close the gap between them. "What happened?"

Without any sign of fear or hesitation, the dog walked right up to her and nuzzled his head into her outstretched hand.

"Well, you're a friendly fella, aren't you?"

The tail gave a brief swish as Toni scratched behind the dog's ear then ran her other hand down the length of him. Or her. No collar. No tangles of fur. Thin but not skeletal. The dog had either been on its own a while and knew how to care for itself or had a miserly master. When she let her hand glide gently over the leg the dog seemed to favor, the friendly pup let out a small whine.

"Okay, looks like we're going to have to find you a vet. I just happen to know where there's a very good one."

The dog, eating up all the attention, shifted and rubbed against her. She understood exactly how the poor dog felt. Loneliness sucked.

CHAPTER TWO

etty Sue and Paul had stayed a couple of hours while Brooks and Nora made sure all was well with Paul Junior's arrival, but the young family went home almost an hour ago. With no appointments scheduled for the rest of the afternoon and the melancholy of Liza's death lingering, Nora insisted he head out to the ranch and work off some steam. The idea was a good one.

Studying medicine may have taken him away from home for most of his adult life, but his heart had always been on the ranch. Even now, he wished he could convince some of his brothers to play hooky from work and hunt frogs in the creek. Or maybe Nora was right, and an afternoon mucking out stalls for his brother Finn would be exactly the mind-clearing hard work he needed. Almost to the end of Main Street, he debated what to do about Meg. Calling her from the ranch made sense—then, he'd be too far away to return to town for dinner. Perhaps by the time dinner rolled around at the end of the week, his soon-to-be sister-in-law might decide her friend isn't in need of a doctor after all.

Even though he'd set his mind to calling after he'd reached the ranch, Brooks turned to look up the street of Meg's new house. Braking to slow down for a better view, he focused on the large clump practically in the middle of the road. What the hell? Pulling a quick u-turn, he circled around and up the street. Adding to the distraction, there was no doubt that at least part of the clump was a person doubled over. Was today never going to end? He hated to believe anyone in Tuckers Bluff would hit a pedestrian and drive away, but that sure as hell was what it looked like to him. Pulling over, he grabbed his medical bag from the passenger seat and bolted out of the car. No telling how long the person had been left, his pace faltered.

A large furry animal raised his head, and Brooks would be willing to testify in a court of law that the creature looked him in the eye and nodded before darting off. What was now clearly a woman sprang to her feet and whirled on him. "You scared him."

Growing up, Brooks knew all the residents in Tuckers Bluff. But the town had grown so much while he was away, he simply didn't know everyone the way he once had, and this lady didn't look at all familiar. "Is he hurt?"

"He's limping."

"Do you know how he got injured?" Brooks trotted across the street. His brother Adam was the vet in the family, but if the dog had been the one hit by a car, the least he could do was help this lady get her pet to Adam's office.

"No. I heard him whining and got him to come to me."

"You're lucky no one ran the two of you over."

Already moving toward the shrubs where the dog had disappeared, the woman turned to look at him, one eyebrow cocked high on her forehead. "In this town?"

"We have cars. What's his name?" Brooks followed the woman in search of her dog.

"He's not mine."

That brought him to a stop. He didn't like the idea of chasing a hurt stray dog. Being bitten by a rabid animal was not on his top ten hit parade. And neither was treating this petite thing for a rabid dog bite. "You better stay here. He could be vicious if he's hurt."

"He's the sweetest thing. I was scratching his ear when you hopped out of that tank and scared him away."

"In the middle of the street." The comment warranted repetition.

Her hands fell heavily on her hips. She rolled her eyes at him, rather big, pretty, ocean-blue eyes, and blew out a puff of air that made her chest rise and fall under his nose. "I think I can handle it from here. Thank you."

His attention immediately fell on the jewelry gracing her left hand. The rock wasn't exactly blinding him, but it came pretty damn close. Too bad. Something about those eyes had sucked him in to a place he had no business going—or wanting to stay.

She spun around and began calling in a soft, sweet tone, "Here, fella. Come on back, baby."

Tempted as he was to do exactly as she'd suggested and turn tail for the ranch, he was fairly sure somewhere in the Hippocratic oath there had to be something about not leaving a delusional woman on her own to chase after a potentially rabid injured animal. "You'd better let me."

"Why?" She spun around and glared at him. "You think he's vicious. Or she. I can take it from here."

The bush by the vacant shop rustled and the petite woman turned quickly forgetting all about Brooks.

"It's okay, sweetie," she cooed. "The mean, big man is going away."

That drew Brooks to a halt again. He wasn't mean. He was a nice guy. A good guy. Everyone liked him. Really they did. The need to suddenly prove her wrong urged him forward. Crouching to half his height, Brooks practically crawled to the shrubbery, "Come here boy, it's okay."

The two of them inched their way, cooing to the now still branches, whistling, and making tsking noises in an effort to coax the animal back into the open.

"I still think he's afraid of you," the woman said in a softer tone and leaned over to look behind the bush. "He's not here." Her gaze drifted along the wall down the side of the vacant parking lot. "I don't see him."

Shifting his focus to the open space, Brooks scanned the immediate area and then did the same up and down the street. "I don't see any sign of him." Raising his fingers to his lips, he blew out a sharp, loud whistle. Nothing. "Maybe he's gone home."

"I don't think he belongs to anyone." She moved farther onto the vacant lot, peering behind all the greenery.

"What makes you say that?"

Frowning, she straightened and faced him. "He didn't have a collar, but it was more his condition."

He waited for a more detailed description.

"I guess the word unloved comes to mind."

"Unloved?"

"You know, not skinny so he's been fed, but not an extra ounce of fat on him. No one to slip him scraps under the table, or treats for a job well done. His coat wasn't tangled and dirty with signs of street life, but it wasn't shiny and soft as though someone took the time to brush him." She sucked in a breath and shrugged her shoulders. "I don't know. Maybe I'm being overly sensitive."

A faraway look, as though she'd gone someplace she didn't want to be, fell across her face. For a brief instant, Brooks was tempted to ask what was wrong. Find out what brought the sudden glint of sadness to her eyes, but that wasn't his place. That honor belonged to the guy who'd given her that rock. "Well, I'll walk around the block, see if he's nearby. Otherwise, I'm going to have to assume he's gone back to wherever he came from." Something Brooks needed to do too. And soon. He didn't like the instincts this woman drew from him.

• • •

The rumble of an engine sounded in the distance. Before Toni could process how far away it was, the stranger had slipped his arm around her waist and circled her away from the curb. With her mind drifting off into a world of self-pity, she hadn't even noticed that she'd inched back toward the street. "I should find the dog."

"Ma'am, maybe I should call your husband to come get you. I have connections at the sheriff's department. I'll make a call and see if anyone is missing a dog. If they are, we'll find him and see that he gets back to his owner."

Another one of *those* men, the kind who thought a woman had no reason to think for herself and needed a man to lead her by the hand. Been there, done that, had enough.

The roar of a massive pickup slowed to a dull hum beside them and the window lowered. "I see you two have met." Meg's fiancé Adam hung his arm out the open window. "Meg just texted me, she's on her way home. Are you planning on jawing out here all day or coming inside for supper?"

Toni turned to look at the man now staring at her with wide emerald-green eyes. Of course, this had to be a Farraday brother. The doctor. Brooks. The resemblance to Adam was striking. Had she not been so lost in concern for the dog, she would have noticed the similarities. Should have noticed.

Stepping aside to retrieve his medical bag, the statuesque doctor with jet-black hair and mesmerizing eyes addressed his brother, "I was just on my way to the ranch. Thought I'd give Finn some help. Muck out a few stalls."

Adam's brow immediately folded into a studious frown. She had no idea what was so alarming about mucking out stalls, but then again, she didn't know a damn thing about life on a ranch. For all she knew mucking was code for "some important animal on the ranch is in trouble."

The crease remained etched in Adam's forehead. "It's getting late in the day for that kind of work."

There was no missing the dimming of light in eyes that had just looked bright with surprise at her. Her heart constricted at the sadness staring off in the distance. Rather than respond with words, Brooks merely turned to Adam and shrugged.

"I'd better warn you." His expression more relaxed, Adam shrugged back. "Becky left early 'cause Dad and Aunt Eileen are joining her and her grandmother for dinner tonight. If you head to the ranch you'll be eating Finn's cooking."

The way Brooks' face pinched at the thought almost made Toni laugh.

On the other hand, Adam didn't make any effort to hide his mirth. "We're having lasagna tonight. Toni made the sauce yesterday. From scratch. I got a taste. Trust me, you want to eat with us."

Brooks glanced at her, and Toni hefted a shoulder. "What can I say? I'm Italian."

With his gaze shifting left and right over her blonde hair, Brooks lifted one eyebrow.

"Northern Italian," she explained. "It's against my genetic makeup to buy sauce in a jar."

An amazing smile stretched across Brooks' face. Her entire body felt as though she'd suddenly stepped into a warming ray of sunshine.

"Looks like you're having company for dinner." Brooks nodded at his brother.

"Good." Adam leaned back into the cab of his truck. "Want a ride, Toni?"

"Sure." Looking over her shoulder one last time for any signs of the dog and seeing none, she circled the hood to climb in. Brooks followed them in a huge SUV. What was it about Texas and cars big enough to be small houses?

Only a short distance to travel up the block, she barely had time to fidget with the seatbelt when Adam pulled into the driveway and it was time to unbuckle.

"Need a hand down?" Adam asked.

"Nope. I can jump as well as the next guy," she teased. Adam's truck was probably the biggest one she'd ever seen and she wasn't exaggerating when she said jump. At five foot four, if she dangled her legs off the side of the passenger seat she was still over a foot from the ground. Grabbing the handle to her right, she stood on the running board and hopped off. "See?"

"Pretty good for a city girl."

The bright smile Adam tossed her way made it easy to understand at least one reason Meg had fallen head over stilettos for the cowboy veterinarian. But despite his smile's high wattage, it didn't have nearly the impact on her as his brother's broad grin. And that was a complication she didn't need.

The interesting thing about a town the size of a postage stamp was how quickly a person could move from one place to another.

Adam had barely slammed the car door behind Toni when Meg pulled into the drive.

Even if Toni hadn't heard the car pull in, she would have known it was Meg from the change in Adam's face. The polite smile he'd bestowed on Toni couldn't compare to the light in his eyes or the power of his grin when his gaze landed on his fiancée. The guy oozed so much love he could have been a poster boy for a sappy romance, the happily-ever-after stories that sucked all starry-eyed, single women into the idea of Prince Charming, Mr. Darcy, and Richard Gere. Except in her case, blinded by a fairytale, she woke up one day to stare into the mirror at a black eye covered in caked-on makeup and an unapologetic stranger barking from across the room.

"Toni," the soft voice and even gentler touch on her arm startled her back a step. Brooks immediately retreated. "Sorry. I didn't mean to startle you."

"No." She shook her head and waved an apologetic hand. She hadn't even noticed his approach. "I was lost in thought."

With only a nod, Brooks looked over to his brother and future sister-in-law then turned toward the house. The strong silent type. Maybe they grew men differently in Texas.

CHAPTER THREE

"How long till supper?" Adam dropped his hat on a hook near the door.

"As soon as the oven is warm, I'll heat up the lasagna." Toni was halfway to the kitchen, a huge smile on her face. Talk about a 180-degree turnaround. Tying an apron behind her back, she practically danced across the kitchen floor.

"Good. I've been on my feet since five this morning." Adam followed her into the kitchen and headed straight to a foil covered tray on the counter.

"That's dessert." Meg sidled up beside him and slapped his hand. "Don't spoil your appetite."

"The turkey sandwich Becky made me eat for lunch evaporated hours ago. It would take a rhinoceros to derail my appetite." Adam spun around to his brother. "You gotta try these. I don't have a sweet tooth, but these things can hook a man onto sugar fast."

Meg had tucked the foil corners around the tray before Brooks could get a good look, but he hadn't missed Toni's grin at Adam's enthusiasm. My God. She was absolutely gorgeous when she smiled. Short blonde curls framed a face with eyes sparkling excitedly and cheeks flushed a pale rosy pink. His gut clenched and his gaze fell once more upon the rock on her left hand. *Down boy.* The lady was taken, and he'd better get a grip on himself.

"If you behave," Toni shot over her shoulder, a pasta tray in hand, opening the oven door, "I promise to make more."

"And make extra to take to Abbie," Meg interjected. "I think they'd be a nice addition to the dessert menu."

"I don't know…" the bright smile slipped from Toni's face and the somber thoughts from earlier clouded her eyes.

"Is anyone going to tell me what this wonderful dessert is?" Brooks dared to finger the corner of the foil covered tray only to have Meg slap his hand away the same way she had his brother's.

"They're Toni's most famous specialty."

"Famous?" He stole a sideways glance at the tray again.

"Yes." Meg dropped her fists to her waist. "Famous. Back in school kids would sacrifice their souls for those. And she only had three flavors then."

Toni slammed the oven door closed and turned. "Vanilla, chocolate, and red velvet."

"I loved the red velvet." Meg blew out a wistful breath.

"Those minty things were okay with me." Adam eyed the tray. Anyone watching could almost see his mind calculating the odds of stealing one out from under Meg's protection.

"I still don't know—" Brooks started.

"Cake balls," three voices chorused.

All this fuss over cake? Brooks looked from the tray to his sister-in-law to his brother to the pleased baker and shrugged, his stomach rumbling at the savory aromas of garlic and baked cheese already easing its way across the remodeled kitchen from the oven. "I don't know about the cake, but that lasagna smells amazing."

Again a bright smile claimed Toni's face, and Brooks had to make an extra effort to grab his mind before it wandered in the so wrong direction.

"Supper won't be ready for at least another twenty minutes." Toni turned to the fridge. "Why don't you guys go find something to keep you busy."

"Good idea." Meg accepted a head of lettuce from her friend with one hand and shooed the men away with the other.

"Might as well show me what's changed since last week." Brooks dutifully marched after his brother. Since Meg had bought the run-down Victorian, the place had slowly been transforming before his eyes.

"Second floor is mostly done, and we've started on the attic suite." A couple of beers from the fridge in hand, Adam turned into the main hall and out the back door. "I actually think Meg's going to have this place in shape in time for the wedding guests."

"She's amazing. No one thought she'd pull it off."

"Ain't that the truth. But we couldn't have done it without the family's help."

One of the first things the family got together for was to rebuild the rotted wraparound porch and extend the rear area out a few feet. Now the large outdoor area was divided into two sections, one with a table and chairs for dining or card-playing and the opposite side lined with dark green wooden rockers. Brooks almost laughed at the memory of the color choosing process for the seating. Meg had wanted white, Aunt Eileen had suggested that a darker tone of brown or burnt orange would be nice. Like good, legacy Aggies, the brothers gagged at the mention of orange. Their suggestion of maroon almost won out until Becky Wilson, Adam's assistant and long-time family friend, casually mentioned the dark green of the old rockers that had been on the Farraday porch most of her young life. The long since replaced furniture had originally been painted that shade by his mother. Nothing more was said, and yet everyone knew the chairs on Adam and Meg's porch would be painted dark green.

"So," Adam handed his brother a long neck bottle. "Want to tell me why you were on your way to muck out stalls at this hour?"

Brooks knew "No" wasn't going to be acceptable. But he also knew his older brother by two years would be the most likely to understand. "Liza Cannon had a heart attack."

Pain colored Adam's face. "She didn't make it."

It wasn't a question, but Brooks shook his head anyway. "They thanked me."

"The family knows you tried."

For all the good that had done, he could set up office in Paradise and there'd be no escaping days like today.

"Ran into Ralph Brennan at the feed store this morning." Adam took a swallow from his beer. "He was looking very… chipper. Wanted to know if Connor was coming home any time soon."

"Connor?"

Adam hefted a lazy shoulder. "Seems last time Connor showed up for Sunday supper he and old man Brennan found time for a little visit."

"Does Finn know?"

Again, Adam shrugged. "Not sure, but this was the longest conversation I've had with Brennan since his wife passed."

It was hard to remember the friendlier older man who had been their neighbor when they were very young. The first change had come when the Brennan's daughter chose to stay up north after school and marry, but the real blow had been when the old guy's wife passed on. "So he'd made plans with Connor, not Finn?"

"He didn't say, but I got the feeling he was in a hurry for whatever his plans are to begin."

"Really?" Brooks couldn't remember their curmudgeonly old neighbor being in a hurry for anything.

"I sent Connor a text. Haven't heard back."

"Yeah, sometimes it's easier to get word from Ethan flying over the middle of no man's land than from Connor less than a state away."

"You can say that again. Maybe I'm getting older than I think, or maybe it has something to do with Meg, but I'm starting to think like Aunt Eileen. I'm ready for all my brothers to be home, safe, and close."

"Only your brothers?"

"I may not like Grace away at law school, but even I can't find a way to compare Dallas to the hazards of working an oil rig or having terrorists shooting at you."

Brooks blew out a sigh. There were days when working the ER at Parkland felt exactly like being in a war zone. But Adam was right, there was no reason to compare a classroom in one of the poshest neighborhoods in Dallas to an inner city hospital. "If something is happening soon, Aunt Eileen will have the scoop by Sunday supper."

"That she will." Adam downed the last of his drink then pushed to his feet. "I say we head back and check on the girls and dinner."

"Right behind you." Though the way Brooks felt at the moment, he might be better off heading straight through the hall, out the front door, and off to the ranch. Of course, no one ever said he was smart about doing what was good for him—or avoiding trouble.

• • •

"I love this kitchen." Toni popped another tray of cake balls into the second oven. With time to kill she'd decided to whip up another batch to send to the ranch and to the clinic with Adam the next day. "I still can't believe you, Margaret Colleen O'Brien, the girl who couldn't boil water, not only bought a former bed and breakfast, you bought one with a chef's dream kitchen." Or at least Toni's dream kitchen.

"It didn't exactly come this way, but I knew good food, good cooks, and fun kitchens go hand in hand. The bulk of the remodel money is in this room. "

Toni was practically drooling over the commercial, stainless-steel range, the full-sized, side-by-side double ovens, the additional warming oven and the dual commercial-grade dishwashers suitable for all the extra baking dishes Toni had helped Meg order online.

"If your plan is to help me gain a hundred pounds while you're visiting," Meg O'Brian winked giving Toni a thumbs up with one hand while scooping a splatter of spilled batter from the counter with the other, "you are so well on your way." Slowly licking her finger clean, Meg closed her eyes and groaned with pleasure. "You're killing me. And my waistline."

"Somehow I doubt that. You've always been as thin as a rail with the metabolism of a racehorse."

"Well, with you around cooking and baking I'm certainly eating like one!" Meg laughed loudly, and despite her earlier words to her fiancé about spoiling their appetites, she lifted the foil covered corner of the cake ball tray and took a slow, delectable bite.

"Wow. Something smells amazing." Nose to the air like a bloodhound following a scent, Adam found his way to the oven and freshly baking desserts.

"And nothing like lasagna." Sniffing the air beside his brother, Brooks crossed the threshold, filling the room.

Damn these Farraday men had presence.

Adam's gaze fell on the uncovered tray, an impish grin taking over his face. Before anyone could react, he snatched one of the unfrosted morsels and tossed it into his mouth like a kernel of popcorn. "I may have to muck out a few stalls at the ranch myself to work off these desserts."

The oven timer sounded and Meg grabbed the salad bowl and handed it to Adam. "Put this on the table please."

"How can I help?" Brooks inched closer to the counter, and while Toni was distracted pulling dinner from the oven and Meg collected silverware from the drawer, he picked one of the cake balls and popped it into his mouth. "Wow. You weren't kidding. These are fantastic."

"It's my secret ingredient that makes the difference." Lasagna tray in hand, Toni grinned up at Brooks.

Brooks accepted the handfuls of forks and knives from his future sister-in-law. "Man, you have got to give the recipe to Aunt Eileen."

"Wouldn't be much of a secret then, would it?" Still smiling, Toni followed Adam to the dining room. It had been ages since anyone had praised her cooking. She'd forgotten just how good that felt. And how much she liked it.

Dinnertime with Meg and the Farradays had been a world away from the lonesome formality Boston meals had become. Tonight was no exception. The table set and food ready to be served, not only did Adam pull out the seat for Meg, but without hesitation, Brooks eased behind Toni and gently pushed her and the seat against the table. "Thank you."

"Yes, ma'am," Brooks nodded.

"The pan is quite hot still. If you'd like to pass your plates, I'll scoop it out." Meg pushed to her feet and, using a metal spatula, sliced into the baked dish.

"Double for me." Adam held out his plate.

"Mine too," Brooks added.

For the first time in a long while, Toni actually felt hungry. Very hungry. "Mine too."

Meg's eyes rounded and both she and Adam turned their surprise in her direction.

Smiling, Toni shrugged. Boston was two thousand miles away. William was even farther. Here in Texas she could relax, enjoy her friend and the peaceful world she lived in. It was time Antoinette Castellano rejoined the world.

CHAPTER FOUR

"I know there's no such thing as weekends off in ranching." Aunt Eileen tied her favorite apple-patterned apron behind her back. Brooks was pretty sure it was the only apron she owned and saved for special occasions. "But I don't see why you have to be out moving cattle on a Sunday when we have guests coming for supper."

"It's a cattle ranch. Moving cattle is what we do." Finn, the youngest of the Farradays, kissed his aunt on the cheek. "Maybe if the best gate-opener this side of the red river came out to help…"

Smart enough to dip and spin out of reach, Finn barely escaped the thwack of Eileen's wooden spoon. "Don't think you're too grown up for a good swat on the ass."

Finn grinned like a petulant teen pulling one over on the only mother figure he'd known then turned to Brooks. "Appreciate the help."

"I needed the workout." Even after a long hot shower, the sting of overused muscles pulling between Brook's shoulder blades clearly agreed.

"Ditto." Freshly showered and shaved, Adam stepped into the kitchen and grinned. Working with large animals on a regular basis, his muscles didn't appear to be protesting after a day of rounding up rogue cattle and repairing damaged fence line the way Brooks' aching muscles did.

"Dad's finishing up in the barn. He'll be here in a few." D.J., the chief of police when he wasn't playing cowboy with his brothers, kicked his heels at the back door, hung his hat on a nearby hook, and staring at the colorful apron, grinned up at his aunt. "We must be having company."

"Don't you start, Declan James." Aunt Eileen began peeling

the potatoes. Grousing under her breath, she wielded the peeler with gusto. "Raised a bunch of smartasses, is what I did."

"I'm deeply wounded." D.J. flattened his palm against his chest, and taking long strides, crossed the country kitchen quickly, twirled his aunt around as if preparing to do-si-do and, tugging her into his arms, gave her a hard hug. "But you love us anyway."

Sputtering with laughter, Eileen swatted D.J. lightly on the shoulder and pushed away. "I've got a mess of potatoes to cook." She glanced out the kitchen window and back. "You'd better hurry and wash up before the ladies get here."

"Look what we've got." Arms laden with large plastic containers, Meg led the way from the front door. Toni, Becky, and her grandmother Dorothy followed behind.

Aunt Eileen turned to greet her guests. "That better be those delicious cake things."

Toni's face lit up at his aunt's words. "They are."

Toni's smile pulled him in like a kid to a pet store window, making it hard for him to look away. Biting down hard on his back teeth, he forced one foot to move in front of the other and then grabbed the containers from Meg before Adam got to her. Brooks was going to have to find a way to put more distance between himself and Toni for the next few weeks until Adam and Meg's wedding was over and Toni went back where she belonged. To her husband.

• • •

Already Toni had met most of Meg's future in-laws. Aunt Eileen reminded her a little of her own mother. Whether Irish or Italian, big families were pretty much the same. Though just one of two children, Toni had plenty of cousins. Thinking back on her childhood and how distant those once-close relations had become since marrying William, Tuckers Bluff reinforced her belief she'd done the right thing. "Where shall I put these?"

Adam retrieved the additional stack of containers she held and frowned in confusion. "How many people are we expecting?"

"They're not all for tonight." Becky chimed in. "Some are going to the clinic with me for our patients. The few you brought the other day went fast and everyone who tried one absolutely raved. It seemed to take the edge off of everyone's worry over their pets."

"That's what happens when food is made with love." Aunt Eileen waved a peeled potato and turned back to slicing. "They were a hit at the Silver Spur. Abbie says they were a big success with all the ladies watching their weight."

The way Toni's eyes rounded, Brooks almost smiled.

"They're not diet," Toni muttered.

"Of course they are." Aunt Eileen rubbed her hands against her hips, reached over to the tray Adam had set beside her, and taking one out of the plastic tray, she grinned up at Toni, "As long as you eat only one." Then she took a bite. "Ooh. Almonds."

"What I don't get," Becky reached for one of the white iced treats, "is how do you stay so skinny with desserts like this around?"

"I don't eat them."

Just about every head in the room spun around to stare at her.

"Well, maybe once in a while."

• • •

"Oh my God."

The sound of Toni's voice had every Farraday in the room turning. The din of chatter that had taken over the kitchen as everyone crossed back and forth came to an instant hush.

Toni stood in the middle of the pantry gawking at the stocked shelves. "The kitchen in my first apartment wasn't half this big."

City girl. As though someone had un-paused the DVR, family and guests instantly returned to their assigned duty: Becky helping Eileen with the potatoes, Dorothy setting the table, and Meg loading up with Aunt Eileen's canned beans while explaining the amount of food cooked on a daily basis at a working ranch. That had Adam chuckling—the city girl explaining the ranch. The two brothers kept busy carrying the chairs and folding table to the back porch for the card game.

"Remind me," Brooks set a stack of chairs against the wall. "Why is the social club playing cards here on a Sunday night?"

"D.J. told me when he was having lunch at the cafe on Friday, the women were all cackling over the cake balls. Wanted Toni to join them for Saturday's game, but she and the girls were going to Abilene all day. Toni did agree to bake up some more of those cake balls, but the next thing I know, Meg's telling me there's another game tonight here on the ranch."

"You'd think she was lacing those things with crack cocaine the way everyone is growing addicted to them."

"You know how women are with anything chocolate."

"Since when have you become such an expert on women?"

Adam didn't bother answering, he simply grabbed a couple more chairs and shot Brooks a shit-eating grin. He opened them beside the makeshift card table and the smile slipped. "Spoke with Dad this morning. He says Brennan asked Aunt Eileen to help him sort through his wife's things. She said she would after the wedding."

Brooks opened one of the chairs and stopped in place. "His wife's been gone for almost twenty years."

Adam shrugged. "There's no timeframe on grief."

"Yeah, but decades?"

"You remember how Dad was."

"Yeah," Brooks sighed and reached for another chair. "I still remember the day Dad came home and found mom's closet cleaned out. Grace was about a year old, a couple of bulls fighting had broken the fencing on the far pasture, and we'd been gone days rounding up all the strays."

Adam shifted his attention off into the distance. "He didn't yell. He didn't rant. He didn't cry. He just looked at Aunt Eileen and said 'I wasn't ready'."

"Then Aunt Eileen blinked away the tears in her eyes and said 'None of us are.' When she walked passed Dad with Grace on her hip, Dad reached out, tugged Grace into his arms and spent the rest of the evening in the barn sitting on a bale of hay telling her how he courted Mom until she caught him."

"By the time he got to the day they learned Grace was a girl, she'd been sound asleep in his arms for hours."

Brooks shifted his gaze across the side yard in the direction of Brennan's house. "The old guy had nobody after his wife passed. His daughter didn't even come for the funeral."

"She couldn't." D.J. stepped out the back door carrying the octagonal game tabletop. "She was dead."

Both Brooks and Adam snapped around in surprise.

D.J. shrugged. "About a year ago he asked me to look her up. Said it was time he tried again. Turns out she was killed in a car crash years before Margorie passed. Brennan's son-in-law sold the house and moved to Chicago with his daughter."

"The little redhead?" Brooks asked

Adam nodded. "I remember her."

"She was a brat," D.J. added.

"She wasn't a brat," Adam responded. "She was afraid of the horses."

D.J. shrugged off the comment. "Same thing."

"She was a city girl, away from her friends, missing her parents, and terrified of all the big animals," Brooks said. "Can't say that I blame her for being a bit out of sorts."

"You should have been a therapist." Adam laughed. "Maybe she wasn't that bad. Do we know what became of her?"

D.J. shrugged. "My friend got Brennan an address. Don't know what happened after that."

"Must really suck to not know your only daughter died, and not see your grandchild for decades." Brooks couldn't imagine losing touch with Dad or any of his siblings. Even though Connor spent more time away working than home with the family, Grace studied in Dallas, and Ethan was a world away flying for Uncle

Sam, they still knew what was going on in each other's lives. At least as much as Uncle Sam allowed. And there was Dad's Uncle George and his family. They were as close as siblings even if they lived hours away. "What kind of a douchebag is the son-in-law anyhow?"

"That's what I was thinking," Adam added.

"Ditto." D.J. chimed in, paused a minute then asked, "Grace isn't dating anyone special, is she?"

"She hasn't said anything to me," Adam answered.

"Me neither," Brooks added. "But I'm not confident she would tell us if she were."

"Yeah. That's what I was thinking." D.J. blew out a sigh then smiled. "We might have threatened castration to one boyfriend too many."

"It wasn't a threat," Adam added.

"Just a promise," Brooks finished, the two older brothers laughing together.

"Whatever." D.J. moved to stand beside his brothers. "She's not going to marry an asshole. Grace may be hell bent on city life but she's still family. She wouldn't marry an ass like Brennan's son-in-law and cut us all out. She wouldn't."

That much Brooks did agree on. But he worried, just a bit, about what would happen when she finished law school. Last time they talked she sounded intent on staying in Dallas, and he couldn't blame her, he'd done the same after his residency. Even D.J. had started his law enforcement career in the Big D. The allure of the big city trumped the boring hometown every time. And there weren't a lot of places to use that fancy JD with an MBA in Tuckers Bluff. He just hoped, unlike the two of them, that Grace wouldn't have to learn the hard way there's no place like home.

CHAPTER FIVE

"Knock knock." Brook's nurse, Nora, pushed the front door to the family ranch open and stuck her head into the room. "Sorry I'm late."

"Don't stand on ceremony." Sean Farraday pushed to his feet and greeted the family friend half way to the dining room, relieving her of a large, foil-covered bowl. The man had raised all his boys to be gentlemen by example—and the occasional switch behind the woodshed if any intentional disrespect had been uncovered. "Everyone's already at the table."

"Evening." Nora hurried to one of two empty seats. "I lost track of time trying to get Charlotte Thomas to join us."

Standing beside her, Brooks pulled out her chair, and all the brothers who'd gotten to their feet upon her arrival retook their seats.

"She really seemed to enjoy herself that one time she joined us," Nora continued without taking a breath, "but there was no talking her into accompanying me."

"That's the third time she's turned down an invite." Becky scooped out a large dollop of scalloped potatoes and passed the dish. For a skinny thing, Adam's assistant had an appetite like a ranch hand after a day of wrestling cattle for branding and vaccinating.

Nora scooted her chair forward and smiled a silent thank you at her boss. More than once she'd commented on how chivalry was slowly dying except around a Farraday. Leaning back, she whipped her napkin off the table and onto her lap, then eased forward, scanning the crowd as though she were about to breach national security. "Charlotte said she was feeling poorly."

There was no missing the look Becky's grandma and Aunt

Eileen exchanged. Those two women had been friends so long they could almost read each other's minds, made it hard as hell to sneak around as kids. Even now, Brooks recognized the way his aunt studied him. She was looking for a tell that he knew more than he was sharing. In this case, that Charlotte Thomas had visited him professionally. "You know," he locked gazes with his aunt, "even if Charlotte had come to see me, I wouldn't be able to say anything."

"Maybe she's in a family way," Dorothy suggested.

"Could be," Aunt Eileen agreed, still reading Brooks with her studious eye. "That could explain why we haven't seen her around town much lately and why she wouldn't see a need to call on a doctor yet."

"More than lately," Nora put in.

Aunt Eileen's face paled and she skewered her nephew with her gaze. "I don't care about those stupid hippo laws. Is Charlotte being treated for something more serious?"

Toni watched Brooks' expression. She could almost see the battle going on inside him. The strength in his deep colorful eyes actually gave her goose bumps. He blinked and drew in a long breath. "The HIPA laws are nothing to ignore, but if there's something medically wrong with Charlotte, she hasn't come to see me about it."

His answer surprised Toni; she thought for sure the legalities of his profession would take preference over the request of his family. It hadn't and, for some odd reason, that made her inexplicably happy. This wasn't her family. None of this had any impact on her, and yet she felt stronger for knowing he loved his family that much.

"Don't you think you ladies are making a mountain out of a molehill?" Sean Farraday kept his eyes on the chore of slicing his ribeye. "Maybe she's just tired. These last few years, old Jake Thomas had spent more time with his horses than at the feed store. I imagine Jake Jr. has had a hell of a time moving back home and bringing that place into the 21st century. "

"Maybe, but still…" Aunt Eileen pressed her lips tightly together.

"Dad's right." Finn, who hadn't said much yet, nodded at his father. "At first dealing with Jake Jr. was night and day from his old man. Always a smile. Always a few minutes to chat about the family. And heaven knows getting computer-generated invoices instead of Old Jake's chicken scrawl has made the accounting easier for us. But lately, he's reminding me more of his father."

"That's a shame." Aunt Eileen eased back in her seat. "I always liked young Jake. Figured he took after his mom's disposition. I hope whatever it is works itself out soon."

"We all have rough patches," Adam added, sliding his left hand beside Meg's, his fingers curled under and with his knuckles he gently rubbed the back of her wrist. In response, Meg graced him with a tender smile. The tiny gesture of love and support had Toni yearning for what should have been. How had she been so wrong about William? And so blind to what had become of her life?

• • •

"It's time for these old bones to hit the sack." The Farraday patriarch pushed out of his favorite chair in the den and stood before his three sons. "Feeding time for the spring calves comes damn early this time of year."

"And if Aunt Eileen's up late playing cards she's not going to be warming the cabs up for us," Finn added.

"She still does that?" Adam looked to his youngest brother. "I would have thought for sure she stopped doing that."

"Why?" their father asked. "When she first got to the ranch there wasn't much she could do. One morning I stepped outside and the feed truck was running. The inside was toasty warm. Made her feel like she was contributing to the workload. Not that raising you unruly bunch wasn't more work than wrangling a pissed-off bull."

Brooks remembered that day too. His aunt had been rushing around in the pitch black of pre-dawn trying to get some of the days' food prep done before Grace woke up. The time had stood out at first because his aunt never went outdoors before the sun, but that morning, still in her slippers, she'd thrown on a coat, run outside, and then come right back in. Later, after his dad left, she'd stood watching from the window. The rumble of the truck's engine filled the room and a huge smile took over her face. It was the first time he'd seen his aunt smile that brightly since his mom had died. He'd never forgotten it. Now it all made sense to him.

A couple of back slaps and waves later and Adam and Brooks were the last brothers left in the living room. For a couple sips of coffee, the two sat in peaceful silence. Brooks was having a hard time wrapping his head around the upcoming wedding. Eventually, the brothers would all get married. Somewhere they all knew that. But still, Brooks always thought there would be a period of getting used to another woman in the family. One of them would date for a few months. At this stage of life they wouldn't need much more than that to know if they'd finally met the right woman, and then there'd be a bit of serious courting followed by a lot of wedding planning.

A few months ago no one had even heard of Meg O'Brien and now it seemed like she'd simply always been a part of the Farraday household. Maybe that's how a man knew when he found the right girl. Maybe she just…fit. Whatever the case, he was truly happy for his brother.

"You're looking awfully serious all of a sudden." Adam leaned back in his seat. "What's on your mind?"

"You."

"Me?" Adam sprang forward again. "What did I do?"

"You found a wife."

This time, Adam fell back against the comfortable sofa, a grin teasing his lips. "Oh. That. I have to admit, I'm a little surprised about it, but…"

"But what?"

Adam grew serious. "I can't remember what life was like before I saw Meg standing on the road."

Brooks remembered. He lived it now. Ordinary. Routine. Like the chickens, up with the sun, go through the day with an occasional diversion here or there, drop exhausted at night, and then start all over again. Not a bad life. All his brothers loved what they did. Well, except maybe Connor. He only worked the rigs to someday pay for his dream. And, despite most of them taking careers outside of ranching, they all loved the ranch and helped when they were needed. He wouldn't trade his small town for anything. Big city life was definitely not for him ever again.

"What about you?" Adam asked.

"Now you sound like Aunt Eileen."

"Sorry." Adam pushed to his feet. "Want another cup?"

"Yeah. One more and then I'll to have to head out too." Brooks followed his brother into the kitchen. "A piece of Aunt Eileen's crumb cake sounds pretty good too."

"No cake balls?"

"Nah. Too much sugar. Leaves me off my game."

"Hi," Toni came back from the downstairs powder room and paused at the kitchen table. "Aunt Eileen said I could help myself to a little ice cream."

"Not having one of your cake balls?" Brooks asked.

"Nope." She shook her head. "Got my heart set on the homemade ice cream."

Brooks couldn't argue with that. Aunt Eileen's ice cream, along with her pies and canned vegetables, took home most of the blue ribbons at the county fair.

"How about some coffee to go with it?" Adam held out a steaming mug in her direction.

Toni turned toward the fridge. "No thanks."

"How's the game going?" Brooks knew he should have kept silent, let her scoop out her ice cream and return to the back porch, but his mouth didn't cooperate. Something inside him wanted to know more about this woman, even if it wasn't in anyone's best interest.

"I only played a couple of hands. Now I'm just watching. But if you're counting winnings, Aunt Eileen and Becky's grandma, Dorothy, seem to be neck and neck."

"Good thing they only play with chips and not for money." Adam handed his brother a cup of coffee. "Otherwise Meg could be losing the dowry."

"Right. Tell the truth," Brooks grinned at his brother. "How much did you have to pay her to agree to marry you?"

Adam put on a pitiful effort at a scowl and walked away, but it didn't work. There was no masking his smile. The guy was too damn happy.

"They make a great couple." Toni sat down and dipped her spoon into the mound of ice cream.

"They do."

Good manners prevented him from leaving her alone in the kitchen. He repeated that to himself a few times as he crossed the room and took a seat across from her. "You went to school with Meg?"

She nodded. "College roommates. Thrown together by the luck of the draw."

"But you're not from Texas?"

"No. Northern Mass. Live in Boston now."

"You don't sound like Boston." He smiled, hoping he hadn't just offended her, and grinned earnestly with relief when she grinned.

"Oh, I could pahk my cah with the best of 'em. But..." she glanced down, poking at her ice cream. "I guess you could say I learned how to pronounce my Rs."

He wasn't sure why, but he didn't like the way her last sentence came out. "It's nice that you and Meg didn't lose touch."

"That's more because of Meg than me." Her spoon slowed again and Brooks wondered what the hell was going on. "She kept at it."

"Life has a way of keeping us busy."

"Yeah. Life." She let the spoon fall and pushed the dish away. "I should go back out with the rest of the ladies."

"I'll take care of that." He reached for the bowl at the same time she did. It was only a flicker of a moment and barely a touch, but the heat arcing between them from the momentary contact startled him. A pair of darkened, soulful, and very surprised eyes blinked at him. The urge to lean forward and kiss away the surprise was even more of a shock to him than the jolt that had just arced between them. Damn was he in big trouble.

She blinked again, her eyes still wide, but she didn't move. The air between them grew inexplicably thick. Brooks was hard pressed to explain why taking in his next breath was so difficult. Only the piercing shrill of a woman's scream snapped him out of his own thoughts and had him bolting across the kitchen and out the back door.

"Oh, God. Don't move," Aunt Eileen kneeled beside her friend and then screeched loudly, "Brooks!"

"I'm right here. What happened?" Flat on her back, eyes closed, Nora lay perfectly still.

"Nora and Meg were going to walk over to the barn and see Connor's new mare."

Sucking in a deep breath, Nora opened her eyes. "I had the bright idea to take a short cut. Who knew there was a big hole off the side of the porch."

"I did." Aunt Eileen muttered. "But you moved before I could stop you."

"What hole?" Adam asked, now standing in the huddle around the fallen nurse.

"Oh, some critter has been digging holes along the back porch to stay warm at night." Eileen waved an arm in the direction of the nearby edge of the porch. "We need to put up a rail."

"No need. I won't be doing that anymore." Nora blinked at the stars. "I think I can sit up now."

"Hang on a minute." Brooks kneeled beside her, gently lifted her leg and rotated the ankle. "Does anything hurt?"

She sucked in a long breath. "Like a mother."

No surprise there. The joint in question was already swelling to the naked eye. Silently he gave a prayer of thanks that due to the propensity for broken bones in this territory, he'd recently opted to drive his old heap another year or two and, instead, invest in x-ray equipment. "We'd better get you into the office for a couple of pictures of that foot."

"I'm sure all I need is some ice and an ace bandage." Nora extended her arms skyward. "Someone help me up."

All eyes looked to Brooks. With the shrug of a single shoulder, he nodded his chin once to the crowd.

Nora barely managed to lean forward before she winced in pain and stopped. "Okay. Maybe we have a little problem here."

Brooks' gaze shifted to Toni now kneeling beside him. Nora might have a little problem, but the way he saw it, he most definitely had one hell of a big problem.

CHAPTER SIX

"I thought for sure the whole family was going to tag along to town." From the back seat, Nora rested, propped on about a hundred pillows while icing her ankle. "I think Aunt Eileen missed her calling in life."

Toni wasn't sure how it happened, but in the commotion of gathering ice, gathering Nora, and delegating duties, the logistics of moving both Nora and her car had become so convoluted that Toni finally held her forefingers between her teeth and blew loudly. All heads had whipped around to face her, and she calmly insisted she would drive Nora's car. "Why do you say that?"

"The woman would have made one hell of a general."

"Okay, you may have a point there. Until now all I'd seen was the card shark. Tonight I got to see her in matriarch mode and after you fell, well, she did take on that angry bear look."

"I can't believe I did that. I should know better than to walk off path at night. That's a city-girl mistake."

Toni glanced at Nora in the rearview mirror and made a mental note to stay on the path if she was ever at the ranch again.

"I suppose I'm lucky the critter curling up in those holes wasn't a rattler."

"A what?" Surely rattler meant something totally different. Like a nickname for a cute barn cat.

"Snakes are all over west Texas. Why do you think everyone wears boots?"

"Cow manure."

"That too." Nora closed her eyes. "This is so not good. Mondays are almost as bad as full moons. The office is going to be a madhouse." She hissed in a breath and Toni thought she was in pain. "Damn. And the Montgomery triplets are scheduled for their

MMR at 9 tomorrow. Blast."

"Surely there must be someone in the office who can help?"

"Nope. There are more cattle than people in this part of the country and all we can do is family medicine basics. For now, it's just the two of us. I'm head nurse, receptionist, and occasional bookkeeper."

"Well, I can help with the bookkeeping if you need me to."

"Really?"

"Assuming two plus two still equals four, yes really." It had been a long time since she'd put her accounting degree to use.

"Accounting is good. I'm a nurse, not a mathematician." In the rearview mirror, Nora's grin grew as wide as the backseat. "How are you with answering the telephone?"

• • •

Brooks had to be out of his mind. It was the only possible explanation for why at 7:45 in the morning he was at his desk listening carefully for the creak of the front door and the arrival of Toni. Even after hours of tossing and turning and several cups of high-octane caffeine, Brooks still wasn't sure how he'd come to agree to Meg's friend stepping in for Nora.

"It will only be a few days." That's what Nora had said once the x-rays showed no fracture or break. Purple and swollen the size of a grapefruit, walking on her ankle was not going to happen overnight. More likely, with soft tissue damage, Nora would be swinging herself around on crutches for a few weeks. Eventually, she'd graduate to an orthopedic boot, but not before the wedding and Toni's return home.

"What a wonderful idea," Meg had added. *"I won't have to feel guilty leaving Toni home alone."*

Thank heavens Brooks didn't have a sliver of spare time in his schedule today. If there was a god in heaven, and he believed there was, maybe he'd be too busy to even notice Nora was gone and the Italian baker would be in her place.

"Yoo hoo," Meg's voice called from the hall.

Had the good Lord seen fit to cut him a break and send his future sister-in-law to fill in instead of the woman who was taking up way too many of his thoughts? "Back here."

Brooks stood and crossed the room, meeting Meg at his office door.

"The café's in a lull before the next wave of customers. Thought I'd walk Toni over."

"I don't see why." Toni called from the other room.

Meg chuckled. "I guess she has a point. We spoke with Nora earlier this morning. The entire seven-minute ride to the cafe, Nora filled Toni in with information on the schedule, the system, the phones, and how you forget to eat."

"I don't forget." He just didn't have time. The first patient would be in any minute. He might as well follow Meg back out to the waiting room and get the day started.

"Good morning," Toni smiled up from beside the coffee pot, and Brooks decided he was going to need a lot more than caffeine to get through the day. "Fresh pot will be ready in a minute."

"Morning. And thanks."

"Well, I'd better get back to the diner before my boss thinks I've returned to Dallas." With a wave for Brooks and a kiss on the cheek for Toni, Meg turned on her heel and scurried out the door and across the street.

Before he could say a word, Toni held out a steaming cup. "Light on the cream, one sugar. I didn't make it very strong. I hope that's okay."

"Thank you." Apparently, Nora could share a great deal of information in only seven minutes, and he wasn't surprised Toni hadn't wanted to brew strong coffee.

"Arlene Montgomery and the triplets are running late, Nadine Peabody canceled her 8:30 appointment because Sadie is feeling poorly again, which works out fine because Burt Larson stepped on a nail in the floorboard at the hardware store and is coming in for a tetanus shot."

Toni rattled the names off as though she'd been living in this town all her life and not just visiting for a few days. And when did she learn all this?

"I didn't hear the phone ring." Or had he been so distracted he'd missed the calls? No, it couldn't be.

"That's because it didn't." Toni smiled. "Nadine called Adam's office first thing this morning. In turn, Becky texted Meg and Meg told me. Burt Larson is walking here and stopped to get a muffin from Abbie, and Mrs. Montgomery was just running into the café to pick up a boxed lunch for Mr. Montgomery."

"How did you do that?"

Toni's forehead wrinkled with confusion. "Do what?

"Get all those names and appointments right? You're not even holding a cheat sheet."

A muffled laugh came from Toni. "That's easy. I'm Italian."

"Excuse me?"

"Did you ever see the movie *My Big Fat Greek Wedding*?"

"Who didn't?"

"Well, it might as well have been *My Big Fat Italian Wedding*. The lead in the movie had her uncles, aunts, cousins, and nieces all named Nick or Nicki. I have an Uncle Angelo, an Aunt Angela, a cousin Angie, and a niece Angelina. Even though I only have one sibling, I have more first cousins than I can count on my fingers and toes. From an early age, if there's one thing a good Italian can manage besides her way around a kitchen, its names and drama."

He wasn't sure he was ready for a lesson on drama. At least not before a few more cups of coffee. But there was no decision to make. The door opened and Burt Larsen came in. The day had begun.

● ● ●

Putting on a brave face first thing this morning and coming in to work with people had taken an Olympic effort at mental calisthenics. It had been a very long time since she'd been this busy or surrounded with this many people. And she loved it.

"I swear that man has the best bedside manner." Fishing in her purse and juggling a baby on one hip, the woman in front of her smiled. "Used to have to go to Butler Spring for tending to, and to boot the doc-in-a-box there tends to be a bit on the surly side. Not Doc Farraday. He's awfully easy on the eyes."

Keeping *her* eyes on the file Brooks had handed her, even if she agreed with the woman, there was no way Toni was saying so. "The doctor would like to follow up with Jason in two weeks. Do you want to make that appointment now?"

"Sure thing."

Toni scheduled the visit, proud of herself for only needing to call Nora once with a refresher course on the computer program Brooks used. Managing the office was proving to be easy and fun. And, since she was limited on how much she could help Brooks, after her next break she was going to take a look at the books.

As soon as the door closed behind the last morning patient, Toni pushed to her feet and made her way to the small kitchen behind the waiting room. One of the things Nora had told her was that Brooks would forget to eat. Apparently, it was a bad habit both Brooks and Adam shared, and one that Nora and Becky did their best to correct. From what Toni could see Nora was absolutely right. For most of the morning, Toni had stayed out at the desk dealing with the patients coming and going and perusing through the spreadsheets. Nora was right about something else— math wasn't her strong suit. A couple of times Toni had needed to stay in the exam room with Brooks. Once when the hypodermic-phobic patient needed a hand to hold while Brooks drew blood, and another time when he needed her limited assistance suturing the gash on a little boy's foot.

Not once did she see Brooks take a detour from the short distance between his office, or exam room, or the front desk into the tiny kitchen that substituted mostly for a lab. Not that it mattered. She came prepared.

"Excuse me." Dish in hand, she tapped lightly at the office door.

Seated behind a large wooden desk, Brooks barely lifted his gaze to meet hers. "Next appointment here early?"

"No." She advanced into the room.

Brooks' gaze dropped to the dish in her hand, and Toni swore she saw a glimmer of a smile before his expression went blank again.

"It's lunch time. You only have thirty minutes until the first afternoon appointment. I thought a chicken cutlet parmesan sandwich would be a nice balance of carbs and protein to get you through the afternoon without making you sleepy."

This time, a smile tipped his lips upward. "Thank you. But you didn't have to go to the trouble. I'm sure we have something in the fridge."

"Yogurt and something that may have been chicken salad in its former life."

Brooks laughed, reached for the napkin she'd laid in front of him next to the plate, and she wondered when exactly had William stopped enjoying her cooking in favor of takeout.

Brooks took his first bite and muffled a satisfied groan. "This is fantastic."

It shouldn't have made her feel so happy that he liked it, but it did. A lot. "Glad you think so."

She'd barely spun on her heel when he asked, "Are you eating something?"

"I brought a sandwich for me too."

"Why don't you pull up a chair and join me?"

Nora said that she usually left Brooks alone to eat and catch up on his morning paperwork and charts, but Toni was glad to sit and visit. She was curious to learn more about this Farraday brother. Probably too curious. "Okay, thank you." She only needed a moment to gather her plate and drink and rejoin her temporary boss.

"You've done really well out there. Thank you."

"You're welcome. It's been fun."

"Have you worked in a doctor's office before?"

Something about the question struck her as funny. Maybe because she was so far out of her skillset, or maybe because working for a living and being married to William Bennet didn't go hand in hand. "No. I'm an accountant by trade."

"By trade? Do you not do accounting anymore?"

"My husband makes a good living."

Brooks kept his gaze on hers. She could see he was waiting for more, but she wasn't all that sure she was ready to share the nightmare her life had become.

CHAPTER SEVEN

Masochist was the first word that flashed into Brooks' head as he waited for Toni to say more about her husband. Or maybe that was just the lesson he needed to hear. More than the ring on her finger, a real picture of the man Toni was married to. The man she belongs to. The reason Brooks needed to do a better job of reeling in his...what...feelings? He couldn't possibly have feelings for Toni; he'd barely met her and certainly didn't *know* her. But like a damn beacon, the kind flashing in the pitch of night to help search and rescue locate a lost sailor, he couldn't squelch whatever survival instinct kept him gravitating toward this woman.

It took a few more seconds to crawl out of his own thoughts and notice her downcast gaze. But even more distressing was the way she'd lowered her sandwich and had begun picking away the edges of lettuce protruding from between the slices of bread. It took another second to realize she wasn't wearing her ring. "What does your husband do?"

Her fingers stilled. "Engineer. He's senior partner in one of the largest privately owned civil engineering firms in the country."

A statement like that would usually be accompanied by a prideful expression. Instead, she continued to stare down at her plate. One more thing he didn't like. Multitudes of questions tumbled about in his head. None of which drew pretty pictures for answers. "You said you're an accountant?"

Her eyes met his and one corner of her mouth almost tilted upward. "My father used to say it wasn't enough to get a degree, I needed a career. Accounting seemed easier than medical school."

"Not for me," he deadpanned without thinking.

Her eyes widened in surprise and then lit with humor. "Not

good at math?"

"Not bad, but it bored me to death."

"There is that." She nodded and took a small bite of the sandwich. He was glad to see the darkness that had suddenly fallen on her break away. "I don't mind the numbers. I like finding balance in things."

"There is that," he mimicked, delighted to see her smile broaden. "So what do you do with your time when you're not rescuing doctors with broken nurses?"

Her gaze dropped again and he wished he'd kept his mouth shut. When her eyes lifted to meet his, the light had dimmed again. "Not much now." Her gaze flicked toward the window and back, and then to the door and back. "The first year we were married I worked for a midsize accounting firm. It was a good fit for me. Felt more like family than work." She set her half-eaten sandwich on the desk. "William didn't like coming home to an empty house. Not that it happened often, but sometimes at month's end I'd have to work late. Since we wanted to start a family I turned my attention to volunteer work. It was easier to control my schedule."

"What kind of volunteer work?"

Her face brightened a bit. "My favorite was teaching cooking classes at the rec center's after school program. The center had a great deal of sporting activities for the athletic kids and computer access for the geeks, but the kids in the middle were harder to keep busy. Cooking is something everyone has to do at some point. Even the boys."

"I'm very proficient with a microwave." He grinned at her. The truth was Aunt Eileen had taught all the siblings to cook, but nothing in a med student or resident's life meshed well with taking time to cook. "You said was?"

"I don't volunteer anymore." She pushed to her feet and flashed a strained smile. "Your next client should be here any minute. I'll take care of the dishes."

"I can clean up." Another thing his aunt taught all the boys.

"No problem. Call me crazy, but I don't mind tidying up a

kitchen. I guess it's that balance thing again."

Before Brooks could decide if she had a point or was crazy to enjoy cleaning, Toni was halfway down the hall. Thirty minutes and the only thing more he'd learned about her was that something, somewhere, had hurt her very badly—and he didn't like it one damn bit.

• • •

"You worked all day today too," Meg emptied the dishwasher. "You really don't have to cook on top of that."

"I like it. You know that." Toni spun around, waving a spice jar at Meg. "It's very likely genetic."

"I doubt that." Meg whiffed the air. "Mom is half Italian. Yet we're both allergic to the kitchen."

Meg said that with such a straight face that Toni couldn't help but laugh with her. The day had been fun. Despite churning up her past, even the lunch break had been a treat. The real mood booster was that Toni felt she was actually making a difference. Being able to correct the accounting and balance the spreadsheets for Nora reminded her that she was capable of so much more than the narrow life she'd been relegated to in Boston. Add that she'd be continuing to help Brooks with the office for at least a couple more days, and she was the happiest she'd been in a very long time.

"You're smiling again. What's up?"

"I'm just happy to be here with you."

Meg pushed the dishwasher door shut and moved closer to the stove. "I'm glad you came too. I missed you."

Spinning in place, Toni wrapped her friend in a grateful hug. "Me too."

"Are you ever going to tell me what happened?" Meg pulled back, her gaze studying Toni carefully.

"I don't know what you mean?"

"We went from friends who constantly chatted back and forth, to short and curt calls or messages, to a polite Christmas card once a year. Now, thankfully, you're back as though nothing had changed between graduation and my wedding. To boot, whenever I ask about your life all these years, I get a litany of your husband's accomplishments. It's almost like you haven't had a life of your own."

Toni gave the simmering pan another stir. Meg was right. Slowly William had whittled away at her until he was her whole world. In less than a week, her once-upon-a-time best friend nailed it, and yet it had taken Toni years to finally see the same thing. "Honestly, I still don't understand what happened myself." Setting the wooden spoon aside, she turned to face Meg again. It was time to tell someone what was really going on in her life. "I've filed for divorce."

Meg's eyes flared into perfectly round circles. "What?"

"Hey." The sound of Adam's boots knocking at the back door drifted into the kitchen. "How are the two prettiest girls in Tuckers Bluff?"

Meg continued to stare at Toni until Adam pulled her into the circle of his arms and then, as seemed to be his routine whenever he came into a room with Meg, he tugged her into their own private world.

Rubbing her hands at her side, Toni redirected her attention to the pots on the stove. Every time her old friend melted into Adam for a hello kiss, Toni felt like a voyeur. And even worse, she was jealous. Jealous of the days when William had eyes for only her. Of a time when she'd been treated like a princess showered with flowers and candlelight dinners and pretty words and smiling faces and promises of happily ever after. And she had been happy. Deliriously happy. For a while. A short while. Very short.

"I hope you're leaving all these recipes with Meg?" Adam released his hold on his fiancée and walked the rest of the way into the kitchen of the old bed and breakfast.

"Absolutely."

Meg stood behind Adam rolling her eyes. The gesture brought Toni back from the chilled place her thoughts had once again led her, and plastered on a thin smile. "But your aunt Eileen is one hell of a good cook."

"She is," Adam agreed. "But she cooks for ranchers. Casseroles and dishes that stick to your ribs after you've been working with cows and bulls and fences and broken down trucks all day long. On the other hand, you could open a fancy restaurant if you wanted."

"I don't want." Cooking for profit would take all the fun out of it. Making meals for people she loved was one thing. Working in a hot kitchen for strangers held no appeal for her.

"A bakery?" he asked, his eyes scanning the counter tops.

"Nope. Not a bakery either, and before you ask, helping Brooks out didn't leave me enough time to make cakes today."

Adam patted his waistline. "That's probably a good thing."

The squeak of the front door opening had Meg and Adam looking at each other in a silent question before Adam moved away, lifting a finger at Meg directing her to remain in the kitchen. The protective gesture surprised Toni; it wasn't like they lived in a crime-ridden big city, and yet, at the same time Adam's immediate response resuscitated the feelings of life with a real prince. Meg was so damn lucky.

"Anyone home?" the deep voice had a familiar timber but when Toni looked to Meg, her friend shrugged and shook her head.

"What the hell are you doing here?" Adam's voice carried into the kitchen along with the sharp sounds of backslapping. A second later Adam and what had to be another Farraday brother waltzed into the kitchen laughing.

Too bad Toni wasn't a reality TV producer. Standing at well over six foot with dark wavy hair and sporting a sun-cloaked tan that surrounded forest green eyes, this guy was worthy of his own TV show. Add the rest of the Farraday clan and she could see half the women in America ogling the real cowboys of west Texas for half an hour every Tuesday night like clockwork.

"Hello," the green-eyed brother extended his hand to her, "I'm Connor. You must be the baker everyone can't stop talking about."

"Toni." She accepted his hand. "And I wouldn't know about everyone."

"I would," Connor smiled wider making the little lines in the corner of his eyes grow deeper and his face even more attractive. "First Ned at the service station, then the folks at the feed store. Everyone had something to say. All of it good."

Toni could feel the heat flushing her cheeks. For too long she'd lived with no one having anything sincerely nice to say to her.

"So what brings you around?" Adam slid onto one of the island stools.

"Decided to sneak into town before my next job. Old man Brennan left me a voicemail that he's ready to sell."

Adam's eyes widened. "Does Finn know?"

"That's why I'm here. I know he's wanted that land for the ranch. Time for a brother to brother chat."

Adam bobbed his head.

The front door creaked again and this time Toni recognized the voice. "Did someone buy a new truck or does that old heap out front mean our long lost brother is bumming dinner again?"

Smiling from ear to ear, Brooks stepped into the room and slapped his younger brother on the shoulder. "I was heading home when I noticed Ruby parked out front."

The oven buzzed and Toni jumped. She'd forgotten she'd set the timer for the chicken. "If you guys can wait another twenty minutes, I'll turn this puppy into a casserole. Should be just enough for an extra mouth.

Connor whiffed at the air and took the stool beside his older brother. "I'm in."

"Don't have to twist my arm." Instead of taking a seat on one of the remaining stools around two sides of the massive island, Brooks came in her direction and stopped so close she could almost feel the heat of his body next to hers. "Anything I can do to help?"

"I'm almost all set. If you'll put that trivet down over there." She turned left, he turned right. Arms bumped and she found herself standing face to face with Brooks and only inches between them. "I, uh ..."

Brooks didn't say a word. He didn't move. His eyes bored into her with the intensity of a high-powered laser that kept her glued in place. For a brief moment his gaze dropped to her lips and then bounced up to her eyes. The urge to ease forward and kiss him was so overwhelming she felt herself teetering forward.

Some semblance of sanity seemed to cut through the invisible hold his gaze had on her and she whirled around to face the counter. Her mind fogged, her extremities numb, and lord help her, her cheeks flushed once again with heat for all the wrong reasons.

CHAPTER EIGHT

With D.J.'s last minute arrival at the house, there was no way to stretch Toni's casserole for another hardy appetite. Hitting the café made the most sense. First to the café door, Brooks held it open for the ladies.

"Thank you," Toni mumbled then Meg repeated the polite phrase more clearly as she crossed the threshold.

"Yeah, thanks little brother." Flashing a cheesy grin at Brooks, Adam followed the women into the town's only eatery.

Without missing a beat, the same way they had done as kids on horseback, in a single, swift gesture, Brooks knocked his brother's hat off his head and grinned back. "Anytime."

"Well," Abbie Kane, the café owner, hurried from behind the counter and rushed to greet the group, "this is a nice surprise. Four for dinner?"

"Six," Adam said. "Connor and D.J. are right behind us."

The words had barely left Adam's lips when the bell over the door jingled and the two additional brothers removed their hats and stomped through the doorway.

"Connor!" Abbie sailed past the group and pulled the younger man into a quick hug. "I'll have to tell Frank to whip up a batch of sweet potato fries just for you. It's been a month of Sundays since you graced us with a visit."

"Been taking on extra work while it's available, Miss Abbie, but—"

"Don't you Miss Abbie me. I'm not old enough to be your mother."

"No ma'am," Gazes locked, Connor smiled at her and for the first time ever, Brooks wondered if there could have been something more than neighborly going on with Abbie and Connor.

Judging by the hint of a scowl on D.J.'s face, the same thought seemed to be crossing his mind as well.

Chairs scraped along the floor as six people accommodated themselves around the big table by the rear window. Brooks hung back an extra moment waiting for Toni to take her seat and then chose to sit at the other end of the table. Ounce of prevention and all that. The rest of his work day after lunch had been like any other day. Scraped knees, flu shots, and joint pains kept him busy. Toni hadn't even come to mind. When she'd left for the day, he'd been so engrossed in lab results, he'd mumbled a polite thank you without even looking up.

If not for spotting Connor's old truck Ruby in front of Meg's place, Brooks wouldn't have stopped. Though if he were honest with himself, if Toni hadn't been staying with Meg, Brooks wouldn't have been looking up Meg's street in the first place. Which was why it made more sense for him to sit on the opposite end of the table from her.

Too bad as soon as he'd sat, Meg pushed to her feet and announced, "The A/C is blowing on my neck." For the next few minutes, chairs shifted and footsteps shuffled until Meg was comfortably situated away from the vents as well as next to Adam. Which meant now, instead of a table length away from Toni, Brooks was nestled beside her.

"I'm really sorry to mess up your dinner," D.J. said to Toni from across the table.

"Coming to the café for dinner was a good suggestion." Toni unfolded her napkin. "My Chicken Tetrazzini can go pretty far, but four men as tall as trees may have been pushing my luck."

D.J. laughed, Connor flashed that smile that usually had half the women in the county swooning, and watching the ease with which his brothers bantered with Toni, Brooks bit down on his back teeth.

"Whatever was cooking smelled awfully good." Connor pointed his thumb toward his brothers. "I'd have been happy to let any of them go hungry."

"I just bet you were," Adam laughed and pointed back at Connor. "Growing up, if you didn't keep your eyes on your plate, this one here would steal the biscuits right out from under you."

Connor shrugged. "You snooze you lose."

As they tended to do at the dinner table at the ranch, the brothers dominated the conversation. D.J. grumbled about budget cuts: "I do not want to have to fire an officer. We're spread thin enough in this county." Adam and Connor talked wild horses: "There are murmurs of moving the herd again. Which we all know is political speak for the weaker ones will wind up as dog food."

But sitting silently, Toni was the one who'd surprised him. Even when Meg brought up wedding talk, Toni remained mostly quiet, though not lost in thought; her attention seemed intent on the happenings across the café.

"So what's the plan?" D.J. asked Connor.

"Don't know yet. But if all goes the way I hope, this time next year I'll be working with horses instead of oil wells."

"Aunt Eileen will like that," Meg said.

"Yeah," D.J. added, "you and Ethan top her daily worry list."

"Working the oil fields is a hell of a lot safer than chauffeuring special forces around a war zone." For a split second, the table grew quiet. It was always hard to be reminded that Ethan's job, piloting a helicopter, wasn't the safest in the military. Then Connor added, "Speaking of our fair haired brother, any interesting news?"

"Same old, same old," Brooks chimed in. "We don't have a clue where he is but he seems to have been reassigned. Last few times he skyped he was indoors and cool. Didn't have that desert feel to it."

"Oh, that would be nice. Maybe they've moved him to Germany or someplace equally safe." Meg already had a worried sister look to her.

"I doubt it," D.J. said. "If he were in Germany, he could tell us."

Each carrying a heavy tray laden with dinner dishes, Abbie

and Shannon, the other waitress, came to the table. They set the plates down one by one. Silverware rattled and napkins waved about as each person prepared to dig in. Only Toni seemed distracted. Her gaze once again settled across the way.

Curiosity had Brooks scanning the restaurant in the direction of her focus. What, or who, couldn't she stop watching?

• • •

In the back of Toni's mind, she could hear her mother repeating, "It's not nice to stare." But she couldn't help it. Something about the lady in the booth at the other end of the café had caught her attention and she couldn't stop looking until she figured out the puzzle.

"Is everything okay?" Meg leaned in and asked quietly, pointing at Toni's untouched plate.

"Oh. Yes, it looks great." She'd ordered the salmon and now wished she'd gone with something less…fishy. Taking a bite of mashed potato, she reassured Meg with a thumbs-up.

"How long will you be visiting?" Connor asked.

Not long enough. "I'm here for the wedding."

Pausing her fork mid-air, Meg looked Toni in the eye. "You're welcome to stay as long as you like."

No doubt her friend's gracious words were prompted by their earlier conversation. The offer made Toni smile. In college, they'd been thick as proverbial thieves. It shouldn't surprise her now to see Meg here for her just like back then. "Thanks."

Once again movement at the table across the way drew her in. Only this time she recognized what she'd seen that she didn't like. It was subtle, but there. Every time the man reached across the table for the salt, or pepper, or this time the dessert menu, the woman with him flinched. The slightest tightening of her shoulders. Toni hoped to God she was reading it wrong, but with every sudden motion, the woman seemed to be bracing herself.

"Is something wrong?"

So engrossed with watching the couple, she'd once again neglected her meal. Only this time the question hadn't come from Meg but Brooks, and he wasn't pointing to her plate but looking at the same table she was. "I don't know," she answered.

His brows rose, wrinkling his forehead. Like Connor's laugh lines, Brooks' furrowed brow only added to his sex appeal. Except like Adam, Connor's good looks had no effect on her. Brooks, on the other hand, leaning in so close, had her stomach doing somersaults.

"Who are those people across the way?" she whispered.

His gaze scanned the general area she'd been watching. "Which table?"

"The booth with the blonde and the man in the white button-down shirt."

"Jake Thomas and his wife, Charlotte. He runs the feed store now. Family business. He came back from Dallas to take over from his dad. Why?" He answered the question but continued to keep his gaze on the couple.

"I'm not sure."

His attention turned back to her. "Yes, you are."

"Maybe." She looked around for some place they could talk in private, but couldn't think of a good reason. What she really wanted was an excuse to get a closer look. "I wish I had a reason…"

Her words hung in the air and when she'd turned her gaze back to Brooks, he studied her for a second then pushed his seat back. "I think I need to walk off dinner." Standing up, he faced Adam. "I'm going to hoof it to your house to get my wheels."

"That's a very good idea." Patting her tummy, Toni shoved her chair back and stood. She'd hit the ladies room before but that hadn't afforded her a better view of the table in question. Brooks just gave her the perfect excuse to walk past the table and get a better look. The walk home would allow her to ask a few questions and kick her ideas around without raising any suspicion. "Mind if I join you?"

CHAPTER NINE

Escorting Toni out of the café, Brooks slowed his pace and figured if the lady wanted a closer look, then a closer look is what she'd get. And maybe he'd figure out what had her so captivated.

"Hey, Jake," Brooks paused at the foot of the table. "Sorry I haven't had a chance to stop by the feed store with a proper welcome home."

"No worries." Sporting a huge smile, Jake Jr. slid out of the booth and extended his hand to Brooks. "I've already had most of the Farradays come through and your aunt has got us stocked with enough home-canned goods to get us through two winters."

"Glad to hear it." Smiling, Brooks turned to Jake's wife. "How are you liking Tuckers Bluff so far?"

"She's just loving it," Jake answered, still smiling like the grand prize winner at the state fair. "Aren't you, hon?"

The petite blonde nodded, her gaze not quite meeting Brooks'. "It's a lovely town."

"Yes, sir. We're delighted to be back home. Houston is okay to visit, but it's not home. Know what I mean?"

"Sure do." He wasn't feeling all that inclined to visit either. "How long you been home now?"

"Almost two months."

"Wow. I really have been remiss. We'll have to get a few of the guys together for a beer and share inflated high school memories."

Jake let out a deep belly laugh and slapped Brooks on the shoulder. "Where the Farradays were involved, no need for inflating. Damn we had some good times together."

"Yeah," Brooks smiled back. "We did. Definitely have to

hang out over a beer."

Jake shook his hand again and retook his seat. "Sounds good. Maybe this weekend."

"I'll see who's free." Stepping away from the table with a wave and angling towards the door, Brooks almost reached for the small of Toni's back but caught himself just in time.

"You know him well?" Toni asked the second the café door had closed behind them.

"Once upon a time. This is a small town the kids all hung out together even if there were years between us. I think Jake is with Connor. I know he's younger than me. Anyhow, he moved away a while ago."

"Sounded like his wife's not from here." Toni fell in step beside him on the sidewalk.

"I'm not sure where she's from. On a visit home—I think I was still a resident—Aunt Eileen mentioned Jake Jr. had gotten married."

"So that was a while ago?"

He slowed his gate to match hers. "Yeah, I guess so. Why? What are all the questions for?"

"He seemed happy, friendly. Almost too happy." She'd slipped her hands in her pockets and averted her eyes.

"I don't know. He was always laughing and joking. One step up from the class clown."

"Not mean?"

"Jake?" Reaching out, Brooks gripped her arm, brought her to a halt, and paused to look at Toni. Her expression was blank, but he could almost see the gears in her mind turning. "What are you thinking?"

Gently pulling her arm back, she continued to walk slowly forward. "Did you notice that he answered for Charlotte?"

Had Jake? The guy had always been very gregarious in school. The life of everyone's party. "I guess not."

"He did. You asked how she liked the town and Jake answered she loved it."

"And…?"

"His wife barely got in a word."

"Well, that's not a surprise, we've never met before. Maybe she's shy."

"Maybe, but I think it's more than that."

Brooks ran the short conversation through his mind again. It played out like a dozen other polite conversations between a couple of guys who hadn't seen each other in years. A few laughs, a few memories, and the required polite invitation that would probably never come to pass.

"I've seen it before."

"Seen what?"

"The gregarious guy, everyone's friend, could charm a nun out of her panties or a king out of his castle. Marries the pretty girl, the nice girl, the girl with big dreams. Slowly her dreams become his dreams."

"That isn't always a bad thing. A man and wife should be able to share a dream."

"Share, not squelch. Her friends, the people she thought closer than blood, get quietly pushed away until her only friends are his friends. Soon she has no dreams, no friends, no voice. He thinks for her, he dreams for her, he speaks for her."

Toni's gaze remained focused down Main Street, but Brooks kept his attention on her and the picture she painted. The depth of her words had the hair on his arms standing on end.

"Then, one day when she's late with supper, or didn't mend a loose button, or maybe forgot to take his lucky suit to the cleaners, the jovial prince shows a darker side and she finds herself cowering every time he raises his voice."

"And his hands?"

"That comes later. After she's thoroughly and completely convinced that whatever is wrong in her world is her fault. If only she were faster, smarter, prettier, funnier. Even things she excelled at seem to elude her. Then a strong grip of the arm and harsh shaking that leave purple welts can only be her fault. Next time she'll be smarter, funnier, faster. She'll do better and there won't be any welts. Did you look at her face?"

His fingers curled into fists at his sides, Brooks blinked. The question unexpected. "I saw her."

"So did I. Want to know what I saw?"

Brooks nodded. They'd just walked past the turn off to Meg's B&B but he remained silent.

"Broken dreams, lost hope, and fear. But that's not the worst of it."

He braced himself for words he didn't want to hear.

"I saw makeup."

"Makeup?" He didn't understand. All women wore makeup.

"Her left cheek, she only turned her head far enough to see it once. A thick layer of cover up and blush. Not the ordinary cover up a woman uses to hide a sleepless night or a few age spots. The heavy-duty kind actors use to hide tattoos and other blemishes. The sort of makeup a wife would buy to hide from outsiders that her husband isn't the nice charming prince the rest of the world believes him to be."

"Jake?" The guy he'd known in school would go out of his way to avoid stepping on an ant. Toni had to be mistaken. "Sometimes things aren't what they seem."

She came to a halt at the corner. Looked over her shoulder at the street sign and back to where they should have turned. "Things are rarely what they seem which is why I know I'm right. Charlotte Thomas is in trouble."

He didn't want to believe it. Didn't want to think anyone he'd known and liked could become someone he couldn't abide. Didn't want to accept that the ugliness he'd left behind in Dallas could spring up so easily here in his little slice of heaven. Didn't want to think how as a healer, the one who was supposed to report spousal abuse to authorities, and had done so more times than he wanted to remember, could have missed the laundry list of signs that Toni had presented him with. And worse, he didn't want to know why Toni was so well-versed in the methods of an abuser. "How can you be sure?"

Eyes narrowed, her gaze leveled with his. Instead of the sadness he'd seen creep into her eyes before, these deep blue orbs stared at him with determination and anger. "Because I was her."

• • •

Had she actually spoken those words? A short while ago she wouldn't have noticed the Charlotte Thomas's of her world. And she certainly wouldn't have admitted that she was one of them. Toni crossed her arms and brushed the chill away. "I've never said that out loud before."

Even though the chill running up her spine had little to do with the temperature dropping alongside the spring sun, Brooks removed his denim jacket and eased it on her shoulders. For the longest few seconds of her life, his fingers rested cautiously on her shoulders. At one point she felt sure he was going to pull her into a comforting embrace, a warmth she desperately needed. But instead he retreated a step. "We should get you inside. The night air is about to descend like a block of ice."

Standing perfectly still, the gap between his next words was so long, Toni wondered if he could possibly have lost his way.

"If you want to talk some more," he lifted his chin and pointed to a gray and white single story house caddy corner from where they stood, "that's my place there. Or we can go back to Meg's."

It took all of five seconds for her to know she had to tell someone what was going on and, despite her earlier declaration to Meg, Toni simply wasn't ready to share what a fool she'd been with her long ago best friend. She was no more capable of sharing her failures with her friend than Toni had been at revealing the truth of her world to her family. Her mother still believed that Toni's fashionable upscale life was what kept her away from family events and accepting calls. Until recently, even Toni hadn't been willing to face her reality. "Your place, please."

A curt nod of his head and placing his warm hand on the small of her back, he nudged her across the road and up the stone path to the old craftsman home. "It's a little sparse, but it's clean."

Based on what Meg said about the amount of time Brooks spent at work and then driving around the county tending to those who couldn't come to him, it was no wonder the sparse but clean home was picture perfect. She'd call it Bachelor 101. Clean lines, dark colors, massive television. And not a speck of dust. "This is nice."

"Thanks." The man had his phone in hand and was dragging his fingers across the front. "Letting Adam know you're here so Meg doesn't worry. Want something to drink?"

"Good idea. And, no thanks."

Another nod and the two shuffled awkwardly in the middle of his living room until he waved at a nearby chair. "That's the most comfortable."

And most likely his favorite chair. "On second thought, tea sounds really nice."

"I'll put on a kettle."

"You have a kettle?" She followed him into the kitchen. Unlike the sleek living room, the kitchen was closer to original, maybe with a fresh coat of paint.

"Honestly?"

She nodded.

"This will be its inaugural brewing." He bit back a smile that worked ten times better than his jacket at making her feel warm all over. And oh so very safe.

"What are we going to do about Charlotte Thomas?"

Box of tea in hand, Brooks closed the cupboard and faced her. "I don't know yet. Tell me more."

"She flinched whenever her husband reached for something."

"I mean about you."

"Oh." She needed something to do. Pulling open a nearby drawer, she found silverware and set it on the tile counter. "I guess you could call me the frog in a pot of cool water."

"Excuse me?"

"If the farmer were to dump a frog in a pot of boiling water the frog would be smart enough to jump out and get away. But if the farmer tosses the frog into a pot of cool water and slowly turns up the heat, before he knows what hit him, the frog is cooked." She blew out a sigh. "I feel like an idiot."

"You're not an idiot. Far from it."

"Everything I said before was true. William was the answer to any girl's dream of Prince Charming. Caring, thoughtful, and handsome. At least that's how it felt. I never saw any of it coming."

"Any of what?"

"The boiling water. The real William. The controller, the manipulator. He was so jealous. At first I actually thought it was because of how much he loved me."

Brooks set the kettle on the stove and waited. He was good at that.

"One day the doorman in our building smiled at me. Before that I thought love and trust went hand in hand. William concluded the doorman and I had to be having an affair. The whole idea was so preposterous I didn't take him seriously. Even after we got a nice new elderly doorman, it never occurred to me there was a connection." She sat on a nearby stool.

"But there was."

Toni nodded slowly. "So many connections I missed."

"But you see them now?"

Bobbing her head again, she rubbed her cheek.

Brooks' eyes narrowed and his lips thinned. "He hit you."

Bringing her hand down to the countertop, she sucked in a deep breath. "Only once. That was enough."

"Now what?"

"I'm not completely sure. I've been planning since that night."

Elbows on the counter, Brooks leaned forward. "When he hit you?"

She nodded. "Saving enough money to leave a well-connected husband when you don't have a job isn't easy."

"What about your family? Wouldn't they help?"

"Of course." She fiddled with a teaspoon. "If they knew. I don't ever want them to learn my life wasn't the dream they, we, thought I'd be living. But more than that, I'm afraid what William could do to them if I went home before it's all over. If I work this out on my own, they have plausible deniability."

"See." Brooks smiled. "Very smart. Not an idiot."

She was feeling a lot smarter today. "Anyhow, I'd skimmed enough to retain a lawyer when William got called out of town so unexpectedly. It was a golden opportunity I had to take. The timing of his trip and Meg's wedding was too good to pass up. I didn't really think ahead."

The kettle whistled and Brooks pulled away. "And the baby?"

"Baby?"

"You didn't think I'd notice?" Lifting the spewing kettle from the fire, he glanced up at her through long, dark lashes. "Every time I've seen you, you've been to the restroom more often than everyone in the room combined. Last night at the ranch, you turned as green as an Irish clover when Adam waved the coffee cup under your nose, I've never known anyone to put peanut butter on peach ice cream, and tonight you turned your nose at the salmon. How far along are you?"

CHAPTER TEN

"No." Toni shook her head emphatically. "You're wrong. I can't have children."

Nausea and bladder control could be symptomatic of many things. But peanut butter and peach ice cream? "Why do you say that?" Brooks asked.

"Even though we talked about starting a family, I was cleaning out William's desk, helping him tidy up."

The man she'd been describing didn't seem the sort to want help staying organized, but Brooks wasn't going to point that out just yet.

"He had a folder for a Dr. Pendleton. The name didn't sound like any of our regular physicians, so I looked inside."

Stirring honey into his tea, Brooks lifted his gaze without raising his head. "While you were tidying up?"

A hint of a smile teased at the corner of her mouth. She knew she'd been busted. "William often kept small sums of cash in his office. Anyhow, turns out my loving husband had a vasectomy and didn't tell me. So you see, there can't be a baby."

Elbows on the table, folding his right hand over his left, Brooks closed his eyes and rested his forehead momentarily onto his closed hands. Toni was most likely in for a very rude awakening and damn he didn't want to be the one to tell her. Raising his gaze to fully meet hers, he spread his palms flat on the counter and sucked it up. "How long ago was the procedure?"

"About six months ago."

Exactly what he was afraid she might say. "Vasectomies, like birth control pills, or any contraception, are not one-hundred percent guaranteed even if it does have the strongest odds of success. Statistics show the odds of still getting pregnant are higher within the first months following the procedure. There is a slim chance your husband could father a child."

He didn't have to ask her if there was a possibility she could be pregnant, her thought process played out on her face like a stage production. First, her eyes rounded in surprise at the revelation of the odds. Biting on her lower lip and squinting in thought, her mind replayed data only she knew: when or if she and William had last had sexual relations, and when was her last menstrual cycle. When all color drained from her face to be replaced with a bland tone of green, much like the one that bathed her cheeks at the smell of strong coffee or stinky fish, he had the answer to both questions. But the clincher came when her hand fell instinctively to her still flat tummy.

Yeah, a married, pregnant woman had gotten very much under his skin, and now every protective instinct in him was ready to pound the asshole husband responsible for all the gray moods into the concrete.

Wrapping shaky fingers around the warm mug of tea, Toni kept her eyes on the steaming brew. "It was maybe a month ago. Four weeks." She snorted. "Four weeks ago Friday. He'd come home with roses and wine and chocolate and a new Prada outfit. Dress, shoes, and purse. I'm sorry to admit, the sort of empty gestures that would have turned my head when we were dating." She huffed a muffled laugh. "It was an apology for the night before. I hadn't realized the price of a black eye could be covered with an expensive new dress." She tightened her grip on the mug. "I didn't dare…well… the next day I returned them and used the money to retain a divorce lawyer."

The price of a black eye. Right now Brooks wished more than anything that anyone else were here listening to her story. Meg, Aunt Eileen, Nora. Even Adam or D.J. would work. Slow building fury at the idea of any man touching Toni, hurting her, churned deep inside him, and it took every thread of self-control not to shove his fist into the nearest wall.

"God, this changes everything." She still hadn't looked up at him.

Sucking in a calming breath, he asked, "Are you going back to him?"

"No!" Finally her eyes met his. "No," she repeated more softly. "Fool me once shame on you, fool me twice shame on me. My lawyer has been working every possible angle to serve him while he's out of the country in an effort to push this through before he comes home."

"Can you do that?"

"No. Maybe. It depends on the US Embassy where he is. If they even have one." Glancing back at the tea again, she lifted the mug to her lips, then eased it down on the counter. "A baby will tie us together forever." And as before when she'd calculated the odds in her mind, her beautiful deep-blue eyes grew small surrounded by the wide circular edge of white. "Oh my God, he'll have visitation. Joint custody even. Oh my God, what if he does to this child what he did to me?"

With the kind of money it sounded like this guy had, Brooks didn't know if now was a good time to bring up that her soon to be ex-husband might try to cut Toni out of the baby's life all together. Taking in the sheer terror growing in her eyes, now was definitely not the time. "Look, don't get all worked up thinking about what ifs until we know what is. Tomorrow at work we'll do a simple pregnancy test. Sound like a plan?"

Her shoulders deflated and her head bobbed up and down in almost slow motion. Waiting until morning to get more answers was going to be slow torture.

● ● ●

Pregnant. The hot tea had done nothing to still her rattled nerves or queasy stomach. For years she'd wanted to start a family. William had always made excuses. One more deal. One more project. Over the past year he'd touched her so rarely, she'd almost given up hope of becoming a family completely. Then about five or six months ago he'd told her it was time to throw away her pills. For all the good it had done. He'd become more harsh, more angry, more demanding and hadn't touched her once until that night four weeks ago. For a little while she'd thought he'd turned a corner, that maybe the shock of striking her, the tears, the black eye, the shame of it all, had brought back the man she'd thought she'd fallen in love with. The sheets were still warm when he'd turned his back and his temper on her. That's when she knew there would be no turning back. For months since the day he'd shaken her so hard he'd left the purple imprint of his hands on her arms, she'd been slowly accepting her reality wasn't her dream. Then after that night she'd begun researching, saving, planning. And now. Lord and now.

"You're worrying." Brooks' low voice snapped her out of her thoughts.

"I don't want to."

"Tell me something fun." His gaze softened and the corners of his mouth tipped up the tiniest bit. "What's your favorite memory of Meg?"

"Driving to Maine at two in the morning for lobster?"

"You're kidding?"

"Nope. We were at a nightclub with a bunch of friends. One by one they broke away and by two o'clock we were losing steam, on our own, and starving. I forget who mentioned the lobster first, but the next thing I knew we were in her car and driving up 95."

"Second favorite memory?"

She tried not to smile too much, but the memory of Meg at the top of the human pyramid bellowing a Tarzan yell that would have given Carol Burnett a run for her money, made Toni snicker with laughter. "We were in Florida for spring break our senior year. Everyone was legal and having a blast. There was this crazy party on the beach. I'd taken a dip in the ocean and when I came up the beach, Meg was at the top of a human pyramid."

"That doesn't sound so funny."

Maybe it had something to do with the mountain of Gator

football players underneath her. "I guess you had to be there. What about you? Who's your best friend?"

"Adam. Outside the family that would be Hank Tatum." This time Brooks smiled. "He and I were the only two from our graduating class to go to A&M. Have some good memories from those days."

"Funniest memory?"

Brooks stared at her for a few long seconds. "Maybe another time. I'd better get you home before Meg sends a posse out looking for you."

Toni hopped off the stool. "Chicken."

"Moi." He slapped his palm against his chest. "This is cattle country, ma'am."

"Okay. I call bull."

Brooks threw his head back and roared with laughter. The thunderous sound rumbled through her, making her want to laugh out loud too. "You, Miss Toni, have definitely got gumption."

"Gumption?"

"Trust me on this." Brooks extended his elbow and waited for Toni to hook her hand through his arm before moving toward the door. "Let me tell you about the time Hank scared the crap—er heck—out of Aunt Eileen. Our sophomore year we rented a cheap apartment in an older complex. The front doors ran along an exterior hall."

"Like a motel?"

"Exactly. Our apartment was upstairs. Dad and Aunt Eileen had come to help us move in. Aunt Eileen took one look at the water roof leak in the bath and the mold growing up the wall and marched down to the manager's office. Half an hour later we were relocating downstairs."

Walking along the sidewalk, Brooks hadn't withdrawn his arm, so Toni kept her hand tucked in the crook of his elbow, enjoying his animated expressions and the obvious love he felt for his aunt.

"So with an armload of pillows, Aunt Eileen is walking on the ground floor toward the new apartment and spots a pair of cowboy boots dangling from the ledge above. A few more steps and she realized the boots now had jeans attached. No sooner had she come to a stop at the dangling boots when Hank landed in a crouch in front of her. She squealed loud enough for most of the neighbors to open their doors."

"Oh my god, no wonder she was frightened. Who expects a man to fall from the sky?"

"Yeah, well, Hank tipped his hat at Aunt Eileen and said, 'Sorry ma'am, it's the fastest way to the first floor.'"

Toni couldn't help but smile. "Okay, maybe I'd like Hank too."

"When they got inside the new apartment, Aunt Eileen told Dad and me what happened. Then, one hand on her hip, Aunt Eileen pointed points a thumb over her shoulder at Hank and said, 'A cowboy finally falls into my life and it's twenty years too late.'"

This time Toni was the one to roar with laughter.

"Yeah," Brooks led her around the corner of Meg's block. "That's how Hank and Aunt Eileen reacted. Dad frowned, I rolled my eyes, but the two of them laughed till they cried. Hank's been like one of the family ever since."

"Now I know I like Hank and I think this seals the deal. I love your aunt. She'd make a great Italian."

"Better not let my dad hear you say that." Brooks slowed his gate. They'd reached Meg's house.

Toni looked up at the old Victorian. "This is going to be gorgeous when she's done."

"And popular. Folks who want to visit around here don't have anyplace to stay for sixty miles."

"Do that many visitors come to Tuckers Bluff?"

"You'd be surprised. We're growing faster than I'd like."

At the door, Toni hesitated a second, wishing she didn't have to pull her arm away. She'd enjoyed the warmth and comfort. Reaching for the handle she paused to look up at him. Deep-green eyes glimmering with laughter seconds ago, stared at her with such intensity that she momentarily lost her breath. If she'd been a teen on a first date, she'd have leaned in and hoped for a good night kiss. But she wasn't a teen and she wasn't on a date and the last thing she needed in her life was another man or another complication.

CHAPTER ELEVEN

For his sanity sake, Brooks descended to the foot of the front porch and waited for Toni to close and latch the door behind her. If he thought his growing interest in Toni was confusing before, every instinct and emotion in him now spiraled nearly out of control. Turning around, he pulled out his phone, punched at his brother's name and at the corner turned right instead of left.

"Hey," D.J.'s easy voice sounded through the earpiece. "Ready for dessert?"

"If I wanted to find out about someone, how would I go about that?"

"What do you mean *find out*?"

"Not the simple stuff that can be found on Google. The stuff the press never talks about. Things a man wouldn't share on Facebook. Anything a man might pay dearly to keep a secret."

Silence lingered and Brooks thought he might make it to the station house before his brother responded. D.J.'s deep exhale was the only sound.

"There are options," he finally said. "Legally, I can't pull information on people for no good reason. And," D.J. emphasized, "my brother's curiosity doesn't count as a good reason."

"You looked up Meg's license plate for Adam."

"Because he said he thought it was a stolen car. That's called probable cause."

"So if I said I thought someone was up to some illegal activity would that also constitute probable cause?"

D.J. let another heavy sigh escape. "Brooks, what's going on?"

"I don't know." Running his hand behind his neck, he shook

his head even though D.J. couldn't see.

More silence settled between them waiting for D.J. to respond. "You're going to have to give me something more tangible to go on."

Brooks reached his brother's door and pulled it open. "I'd rather do this in person."

Esther, the police dispatcher, was at her desk near the far corner of the county office. "Well now isn't this a surprise. The Kelly boys toilet paper your house again?"

The woman's toothy grin was almost enough to make Brooks smile. "No, just checking up on my little brother. Is he behaving himself?"

"He," D.J. stepped out of his office, "may haul your ass in for harassing an officer of the law if you annoy his dispatcher."

"Nah," Esther waved D.J. off. "The doc is easy on the eyes. He can come harass me anytime. Even if his house hasn't been TPed."

"Same here." Brooks smiled back at the woman who had been a police department staple for as long as he could remember.

D.J. stepped aside holding the office door open and waited for Brooks to pass him then closed the door behind them. "If I hadn't come back to the office were you going to walk all the way to my place?"

"You're always at the office. When was the last time you slept out at your place?"

D.J. shrugged.

Brooks knew his brother spent more time on the cot in the back room than he did in his own bed. The guy lived and breathed his job, and some days that worried Brooks. Other days he was just glad that D.J. wasn't a detective in a big city anymore.

Circling the weathered, oak desk, D.J. shook his head and dropped into his seat. "What's this about?"

"Toni."

"You want to dig up dirt on Toni?" D.J.'s brow arched in interest.

Brooks shook his head. "Her husband. And I don't know so much that I want dirt, but I want to know what I'm up against besides his net worth."

"*You're* up against?" D.J.'s palms landed flat on the worn, wooden surface, outrage flaring his nostrils. "Brookstone Farraday, what the hell are you thinking?"

Not what D.J. was thinking. "It's not like that. She's running away."

Some of the fire in D.J.'s eyes at the thought of Brooks poaching another man's wife ebbed enough for his expression to turn thoughtful. "Meg hasn't said anything to me, she would—"

"Meg doesn't know."

D.J.'s brow inched up again. "But you do?"

"Look, I'm not interested in an inquisition. She's lived through a long history of emotional abuse that recently became physical, and she's bolted."

"Here?"

Brooks nodded.

"Isn't her husband supposed to be out of the country?"

Brooks nodded his head again.

"Which is why she's running away." D.J. ran his fingers across his forehead. "Damn, I hope this isn't going to become a family tradition. I don't think I'm up to any more future sister-in-laws running away from crazy-ass men and hiding out in Tuckers Bluff."

"Who said anything about future sister-in-laws?"

"Abbie."

"What?"

"When I was paying the bill for dinner, Abbie mentioned in passing what a shame you hadn't met Toni first, that you two made a nice couple. I didn't think anything about it, but buddy, sitting here now talking to me about her…"

"Yes?"

"You've got the same look Adam had. And if what you say about her husband is true…" he let his words hang.

"Now you're seeing things." Yes, Toni had gotten under his skin, and yes, he was mad as a penned bull over what she'd told him about her marriage, but he didn't care what the café owner thought, he wasn't head over boot heels in love with anyone. "So can you help?"

"I've still got contacts in Dallas, but all we'd get is mostly surface info. How badly do you want to dig deep?"

"Remember Mr. Tatum's old Mustang convertible?"

"The one you spent six months saving for and drove us all crazy pining over?"

Brooks dipped his chin. "I want this more."

"Okay." D.J. blew out a sigh. "But what I have in mind probably won't come cheap."

Brooks thought about the next wave of purchases he'd had his eye on for the lab. Then he thought about what could happen if Toni proved to be pregnant, which he was pretty damn sure she was and if, like a bad made-for-TV movie, the asshole husband had the wherewithal and connections to keep the child away from her. "That's fine."

"Back when I was stationed in Afghanistan we had a run-in with a prisoner and rather... dubious protocol."

Brooks didn't want to know what that meant, but he had a feeling it involved just the sort of rule-breaker he was going to need.

"I got pretty friendly with a couple of the SEALs who brought him in. One in particular now has a security company in Florida. The guy's top notch. And he goes out of his way to help veterans."

"I'm not a veteran."

"I am."

Brooks had to smile. There'd been no doubt that his brothers would back him up in anything. *Farradays stand by Farradays.* Honor was everything to a Farraday. Family was even more. Still Brooks wasn't the one in trouble, and technically Toni was nothing to any of the Farradays, but if it mattered to Brooks it mattered to his brothers. "Thanks. Now what?"

"His name is Brooklyn."

He thought SEALs usually had tough monikers like Viper or Ice.

D.J. scrolled through his phone. "Rumor has it, between the Navy and starting his own firm, he worked for the spooks."

"Spooks?"

"CIA. Here we go. I'll shoot him a text and see what we can do."

Brooks nodded and watched his brother's fingers work the small screen then tap and set his phone on the desk. His fingers had yet to release the apparatus when it rang and D.J.'s face brightened. Chuckling to himself, he swiped the phone and hit speaker. "That was quick for a squid."

"Gotta keep you jarheads in line," a slight New York accent told Brooks where the SEAL had gotten his call sign. "It's been too long, figured if you're reaching out at this hour it wasn't to rehash old times."

"You got me there."

"What can I do for you, Dec? I still owe you for saving my six in Fallujah."

Brooks wasn't up on sailor speak, though he was pretty sure six was pilot talk for having someone's back. In this case saving his ass might be more fitting. Adding where all this six-saving happened made Brooks think that whatever had gone down with the prisoner in the middle of a war zone had little to do with protocol, and had been a hell of a lot more than dubious.

For the next few minutes, D.J. filled Brooklyn in on what little information he and Brooks had, along with some basic data D.J. retrieved from the database he had access to as they spoke.

"I'm on it," Brooklyn said. "But right now I'd say the lady needs a good lawyer more than anything."

"Next on our list," D.J. answered and Brooks wondered what else his brother had been scribbling on his notepad.

"Gotta run. Baby still doesn't sleep through the night, and it's my turn to do the pat-the-back-and-change-the-diaper thing."

D.J. bit back a smile. "Later." The call disconnected and D.J. continued to grin at his dark screen. "Part of me finds it hard to believe this guy who looked like he'd fallen out of a Rambo movie is playing Mr. Dad, and then another part of me thinks that's going to be one helluva lucky kid."

"Sounds like a nice guy."

"He's one of the good guys. Really good guys. The kind you want to have your back when things get ugly."

"Sounds like that's a two-way street."

"More often than it should have been." D.J. heaved a heavy breath and looked up. "Well, number two son, looks like you'd better shine up your armor and mount your steed. You've got your damsel. Now go save her."

• • •

A cup of hot chocolate in each hand, Toni pulled up her big-girl panties and popped her head into Meg's office. "Ready for a break?"

"Oh, I didn't hear you come in." Closing her laptop, Meg reached out for the cup crowned with a tall dollop of whipped cream. "That looks scrumptious."

"The days seem to be getting warmer but the nights are still pretty cold."

"That they are." Meg dipped her tongue into the cream and blew at the steaming cocoa. "Tea for a long day, coffee for a cram session, wine for an A on the final, and hot chocolate for brace yourself—shits gonna to hit the fan."

"You have a good memory." Toni curled up in the Victorian ladies' sewing chair beside the oversized desk. "This is surprisingly comfortable."

"Women sat in them for hours a day with nothing to do but needlepoint."

"Makes sense." The words of where to start tumbled around in her head. "Things with William haven't been going well lately. I guess a long time actually."

"So I gathered." Meg blew on the brew again. "Your first days here were worrisome for me. You were most definitely not yourself. I actually asked Brooks to come take a look at you."

"You did what?"

"I know," Meg rolled her eyes. "By the time he finally came over you'd been baking and seemed more like your old self."

"Yeah well, my old self is a long ways away."

Meg set her mug down and leaned forward. "If a little time away will help you guys sort things out, I have plenty of bedrooms."

"No. This can't be fixed. Divorce is the only answer." Subconsciously the back of her hand rose to rub her cheek.

"Oh God, no." Meg stared into Toni's eyes. "How long has this been going on?"

"The hitting, not very. The marriage, too long."

"Oh, Toni, I'm so sorry. You can stay here as long as you need. And if you want a job I'm sure Abbie—"

"No, first and only priority is the wedding. You're going to worry about all the bride-to-be business and let me worry about my business. My problems can wait. However, I do think I might take you up on the offer to stay a little longer. You see, things may be more complicated than I'd first expected."

"How can it be complicated? The prince turned into a nasty frog and you've escaped the castle."

Toni closed her eyes and sighed. This should be such fantastic news and because of her disastrous marriage, she was dreading tomorrow's results. "Brooks thinks I'm pregnant."

Meg hesitated. "Normally, this is when I'd be jumping up and down but from the look on your face, maybe not."

"I don't know what to think right now. Brooks said not to think, to wait and see."

"Brooks said?"

"Yes."

Wordlessly, Meg's gaze leveled with hers.

"Well, he is the doctor."

Meg nodded.

"And he's definitely not like William." She'd had enough of men like him. She would never make that mistake again. Ever.

"That he isn't," Meg answered quickly.

"I can make up my own mind." And she could. She might be a bit out of practice, but still…

"I know that. And you're right, stewing all night won't change anything."

"Exactly." Besides, she'd believed in Prince Charming once. She didn't care how nice Brooks was, she would not make that mistake again.

CHAPTER TWELVE

Sleep had evaded Brooks most of the night. The only thing likely to get him through today was a great deal of very strong coffee. Pulling his old Suburban into the café parking lot he looked from the still-dark horizon at the edge of town to the lights inside. Abbie scurried about. That woman worked as hard as any ranch hand. At least a rancher's day ended after dark.

With one of the waitresses still out on maternity leave, Meg would be coming in any minute for the day shift. No sense in sitting in his vehicle contemplating the immortality of the crab.

"You growing roots?" Adam tapped on the closed window.

"Didn't feel like making my own breakfast this morning."

"Don't blame you. I've got a heavy load of ranches today. Need to get an early start. Frank's a better cook than me."

"He's a better cook than most people, but if you tell Aunt Eileen I said that, I'll swear you're lying." The two brothers laughed at the old joke. It was one of those things, like contemplating the immortality of the crab, that their mother would say often. Using her expressions from time to time in his everyday life made Brooks feel a little closer to his mom. Since Adam always played along, Brooks figured it was the same way for both of them.

"Well, aren't you two early birds today." Abbie stopped setting out silverware on the tables. "Coffee will be ready in a few seconds. The usual?"

Brooks and Adam both nodded. The usual was listed on the menu as the Rancher's Breakfast: eggs, pancakes, sausage, bacon, grits, biscuits and gravy, plenty of carbs and protein to fuel a rancher from sun up to lunch. And on long days that kept the rancher and his crew working 'till suppertime like when they shipped cattle, Abbie's breakfast could prevent them from falling flat on their faces.

Situated in Adam's favorite back booth, Brooks looked up just as Meg hurried in the door. Her gaze immediately landed on Adam and her face lit up like a kid with a new pony.

For so long Brooks had worked hard to reach his goals. In college he'd kept his grades high, proud to continue the A&M family legacy. Next, he'd aced the MCATs and med school, landing a primo residency spot. Finally making his way back home, he'd fixed up the old tailor's shop at the other end of Main Street and turned it into the first hometown doctor's office the town had seen in almost a hundred years. Only in the last few months since Meg's arrival had it occurred to him that he might want more than a growing practice and self-sufficient clinic. He'd always known some day he'd want a family of his own, but until Adam had fallen hard for Meg, it hadn't occurred to Brooks that he might want that life sooner than later.

With a pot of hot coffee in one hand and two mugs dangling from a couple of fingers on her other hand, Meg came to a stop in front of their table. "Toni told me what's going on."

Adam looked from Meg to Brooks a few times while Meg poured the hot, black liquid into the mugs and Brooks kept quiet. "Okay," Adam reached for the hot cup. "I give. What's going on?"

Meg slid into the seat beside her fiancé. "None of us really liked the asshole."

"Asshole?" Adam raised a brow.

"Her boyfriend then husband. Oh, don't get me wrong, William said and did all the right things. Brought Toni a bouquet of flowers and always had a bloom or two for me."

"Sounds thoughtful," Adam muttered.

Meg slanted a less than appreciative glance his way. "She was beautiful, smart, made him look better, be better. He'd praised her up and down that I almost wondered if he was developing a Madonna complex. Even with all that, he was too smooth, too charming. But how can you tell a friend to stop dating a guy because he's too nice to you?"

Adam said nothing, and Brooks felt obligated to offer a lazy shrug. She had a point. What could they have said? Though he wished to hell now they'd tried something.

"Then things really changed after spring break. Oh, he still brought the flowers and the trinkets and said nice things, but now there was always an excuse why they couldn't join our group. Always something with his friends, or his family, and none of us were ever included."

Brooks knew where this was going. The frog in the boiling water.

"We still talked after graduation. I even got invited to the wedding. But after that, the phone calls slowed and soon stopped. The only reason I knew where to find her was the Christmas card I still got every year."

"You've described classic isolation techniques," Brooks wished he didn't have to say that. Wished the only reason he knew about abuse was from textbooks. He also wished he could pick and choose the memories that stayed sharp in his mind after his years in an inner city hospital.

"I don't understand why she put up with it for as long as she did. At least she's finally left the good-for-nothing—" Meg looked up as another customer came in. "She and I talked for hours. I wanted to throttle her for not leaving him sooner. Before the control freak got physical."

"I'm actually surprised he didn't become physically violent sooner." Brooks took a sip of his coffee.

Another customer came through the door. Sliding out of the booth Meg whispered, "If anyone had ever laid a hand on me I'd have knocked his sorry ass all the way back to the Stone Age." And with that, she was on her way to take care of the next customer.

"Guess she told you." Brooks recognized the storm brewing in his brother's eyes. Brooks had felt the same frustrated fury listening to Toni last night.

"You know better than anyone that I would no sooner strike a woman than eat manure."

"I know." Brooks smiled. Each and every one of them had fallen in shit more than once. Literally. But Adam was right. They'd both eat cow patties if the only other choice was physical violence against the opposite sex.

"You seem to know all about it."

Brooks nodded. "Toni clued me in last night."

"Rather personal for a woman to share with a man she barely knows before telling one of her oldest friends. Don't you think?"

"I do. But she was worried about Charlotte Thomas."

"What?"

"She thinks Jake's an abuser. And frankly, after listening to her I think she may be right."

"Jake? That guy would go out of his way to help a wounded fly. I can't believe—"

"Jake the kid we knew maybe not, but how well do we know the man who's moved home?"

Stunned, Adam leaned back in his seat. "I don't know."

"I thought I'd talk to Aunt Eileen. The ladies have been trying to get Charlotte into the social circle. She may know something."

"No." Adam shook his head. "If Aunt Eileen even suspected, she'd be after Jake with a shotgun. We'd see our first citizen tarred and feathered and run out of town on a rail."

Brooks chuckled softly. "True. But still…"

"Yeah. I hate letting go of the delusion that nothing can touch our world."

"I know what you mean. But we have a bigger problem."

Adam cocked his head at his brother.

Brooks set his hot mug on the table. "If all we have are suspicions, how the hell do we stop him?"

• • •

Considering how troubled she'd felt even after talking things out with Meg, Toni had no idea why she'd slept like a baby. Unless, of course, baby was the key word. Mindlessly her hand fell to her stomach. What was she going to do if Brooks was right?

Dropping her purse into the bottom drawer of the filing cabinet, she turned to see Brooks coming down the short hall from his office. Why did she feel like she was about to face a firing squad? Brooks wasn't the enemy and certainly not her executioner. "Morning."

"Morning. Sleep well?"

"Surprisingly, yes."

One corner of his mouth twitched upward a time or two before he fully smothered the smile. Too bad, she would have liked the reassurance that seemed to come with one of his winsome smiles.

"If you'll come on back to my office, we'll get this started."

"Your office?" She sure hoped he wasn't planning on giving her an exam because, doctor or not, there was no way she was getting naked in front of him.

"I'll want to get some more information from you and then I'll give you a cup to pee in. It will only take a few minutes for the result. The blood workup will be a final confirmation. But we rarely get false positives."

"Oh. Yes, well." Wringing her hands in front of her, she seriously considered turning and making a bee-line out the front door and not stopping until she reached...where? A tear welled in her eye and spilled over on to her cheek.

"Hey," Brooks stepped into her space. "It's going to be fine. I promise."

The pad of his thumb brushed along her cheek, wiping away the stupid tear. The same cheek that had once stung from William's fist now heated with Brooks' tender touch. "I don't know why I'm crying."

This time, Brooks didn't hide the knowing smile. "I think I do. Come on, let's get this over with."

Twenty long minutes later, Toni sat still as stone waiting for

Brooks to come back to his desk. She'd hoped she'd be able to read his face, but the guy must have spent more years than she'd thought practicing a neutral bedside manner. "Well?" she asked. Instead of taking his seat behind his big desk, he lowered himself into the visitor seat beside her and she knew. "I'm pregnant."

"Mmhm." He didn't move. For a second his gaze dropped to her hands strangling a single tissue and immediately returned to meet hers. "Have you given any thought to what happens now?"

Her head shook back and forth of its own will. She'd thought, but had no idea what she'd thought.

"First thing, I'm going to give you a prescription for some vitamins. You'll need lots of extra nutrients but I don't want you depending on the prenatals for that. I want you to add plenty of protein and green vegetables to your diet."

Toni nodded. Not that she was following what he said, it simply seemed to be the right thing to do.

"The next thing you may want to consider is calling your lawyer."

Right. Lawyer. William. Tears came to her eyes again, not one, but several. In both eyes and they eagerly spilled over the lower lids and ran down her cheeks. "I'm sorry."

Easing forward he pulled her into the crook of his shoulder. "Don't apologize. It's hormones. You may find yourself crying when Abbie tells you the café is out of chocolate cake."

That made her chuckle *and* cry. "Really?" She used the shredded tissue to wipe at the tears.

"Really. But it will all be worth it. You'll see."

His words meant more to her than she could have imagined. Or maybe it was the hormones. But as easily as she wanted to cry, she now felt like smiling. Really smiling. Like a huge banana split with nuts, whipped cream, and extra cherries had been placed in front of her kind of smile. Dabbing one last time at her tears, she pulled back from the semi-embrace and let the grin take over her face. "A baby."

Returning the pleased grin, Brooks nodded.

"A real one." God, had she really said something that stupid? She must have because Brooks chuckled and nodded. "Wow." Resting her hand on her tummy, she glanced up at Brooks' still smiling face. "We're having a baby."

Brooks' smile slipped. And she heard her own words reverberate in her head.

Dear lord, what had she done?

CHAPTER THIRTEEN

"We're having a baby," echoed in his ears. He'd seen plenty of new mothers overjoyed with the news and too many underwhelmed. But the words this time, from this woman, sliced at him like a precision scalpel.

"I'm sorry. I guess I mean, I am." Her fingers squeezed at the nearly shredded tissue.

Some men were such assholes. Blessed with nice, smart, pretty, and caring women and they turn their fists on them. And now, a child. Brooks pushed the memories from his time in Dallas of broken children crying in the care of social workers as they were taken away from their abusive parents. The lucky ones. The ones who the system uncovered before it was too late. "You up to working again today?"

Toni bobbed her head and straightened her shoulders. "Let's get this show on the road."

His first patient was due any minute. A full morning of simple appointments and a low key afternoon. Folks were early to rise in ranch country. Coming into town and taking care of business and appointments started early too. For the next few hours the only conversation between him and Toni consisted of files, prescriptions, computer questions, and more file exchange with an occasional snack and cup of coffee for Brooks. Even though she was the soon-to-be-mom who needed taking care of, he was the one being watched after.

"Your aunt dropped this off while you were in with your last patient. Thought you might like a fresh cup to go with it." Toni set his aunt's famous crumb cake in front of him with steaming coffee.

"And you?"

A huge toothy grin took over her face. "I ate the bigger piece." And before he could say another word, she'd pulled the door shut behind her. Already he was sure Toni would be one of those women who fully embraced the idea of eating for two. Shoveling the last bite in his mouth at the sounds of footsteps tapping up the hall, he made a mental note to check in with Brooklyn this evening. He had no idea how yet, but he was going to help make sure that bastard of a husband never laid another hand on Toni or her child.

"Excuse me," Toni rapped lightly on the door and popped her head into his office. "Mrs. Thomas is here."

"Adelaide?" He turned to look at his schedule.

"No. Charlotte. And she doesn't have an appointment but if you want to squeeze her in, I can stall your next patient when he gets here."

The next patient was coming in for a follow up on how his new blood pressure meds were working out. Knowing how the friendly farmer loved to talk, Nora always allotted him a few extra minutes. If Brooks cut it short a bit, he could work Charlotte Thomas in. "Did she say what she's here for?"

Toni shook her head. "But her left wrist is wrapped in an ace bandage. And she's wearing long sleeves on a pretty day."

Damn it. Well, it looked like once and for all he was about to find out if Toni was on the money about Jake Jr. and his wife. Despite his gut telling him he wasn't going to like the answer, he still prayed that Toni was dead wrong. "Bring her in."

On his feet, Brooks slid out of his lab coat and placed it on the rack behind his desk. Something told him if things were about to go down the way he suspected, a more casual rapport might be in order.

"Here you go," Toni stood by the door, handed Brooks a folder, and waved Charlotte inside.

"Thank you for seeing me without an appointment," the soft voice said.

"Not a problem. We run a pretty casual place around here."

He glanced at her wrist and the guarded way she held it against her. *Damn.* "Let's have a seat and tell me how I can help you."

Her gaze shifted to the chairs and back. For a split second Brooks thought she might change her mind and bolt, only to breath easier when her foot moved forward.

"I, uh, I think I may have hurt my wrist. I mean. I know I hurt it. I, uh, fell. Yesterday." She gave a meek smile. "Always something to trip over at the feed store."

"I see." Brooks opened up the file with paperwork Charlotte had filled in. The very limited information she'd put down. "No drug allergies?"

She shook her head.

"I don't see any medications listed." He eyed her over the edge of the folder.

"An occasional ibuprofen."

"Taking it now for the wrist?"

Biting down gently on her lower lip, she nodded.

"All right," he pushed to his feet. "Let's step into the exam room and have a look." One of the perks to being a country doctor was having time to sit and chat with a patient outside of the confines of a sterile exam room. Passing through the open door he waved inside. "Climb on up."

Charlotte glanced at the exam table and stepping onto the stool, turned slowly, clutching her arm to her ribs and gingerly eased herself down.

The effort to hide her pain wasn't wasted on him. *Shit.* Placing a disposable cap on the thermometer he placed the apparatus at her ear and waited for the ding. "Good."

Her gaze followed his movements as he put away the thermometer and reached for the blood pressure cuff. Charlotte had already rolled her sleeve up far enough to expose the entire ace bandage. "Good. Roll your sleeve up a little further and we'll get your blood pressure." The way her eyes rounded anyone would think he'd asked her to ride down Main Street naked.

"My blood pressure is fine. Always low. It's just my wrist."

Her eyes darted to the door. "I shouldn't have come. Jake...I shouldn't have come," she mumbled.

There was no way he was letting her bolt. He put on his best reassuring smile and lowered his voice to the same tone he'd use on a nervous filly at the ranch. "No problem. I'm going to unwrap this and see what we have."

Eyes still filled with traces of panic meshed with fear, blinked. Hesitantly, she nodded, wincing with every movement as he held her elbow, raised her hand, and turned the bandage. No matter how gentle or careful he was, his very breath seemed to cause her pain. *Damn.*

Finally holding the exposed wrist, Brooks had no doubt it was broken. "We're going to need an x-ray."

Again, her eyes widened, and her lips pressed tightly together. "How much more will that be?"

"Don't you worry about that. You pay for it later when you can."

That seemed to give her pause. Still nibbling on her lower lip she nodded and eased herself off the chair. Normally, Nora would be the one to help with the x-rays, but not only did Toni not know anything about operating the machine, in her condition, helping was out of the question.

Settled in, he placed her arm where he needed it. "This is going to hurt but I need you to hold your arm like this while I take the picture."

With her arm flat and slightly turned she pursed her lips tightly closed and waited for him to give the all-clear to relax in a less painful position.

At this point, Brooks left Charlotte sitting in his office while he darted between his chatty farmer and the developing x-rays. By the time the pictures were ready for viewing, he'd finished up with the farmer and one other patient, and Charlotte was as antsy as a cat in a room full of rockers. All Brooks had to figure out was how to get her to tell him the truth.

"Well. You're right." He took a seat behind his desk. "You

have a spiral fracture."

Charlotte nodded.

"The line looks fairly clean. It's my recommendation that we immobilize it for now. You'll have to have surgery to reduce it and an orthopedist would be the best to determine if you need pins. I can recommend—"

"No." Charlotte shook her head fast and hard. "I can't go anywhere. I... I just need you to put a cast on it, please. I'll take care of it. I promise. It will be all right."

"It would be best—"

"No."

"Charlotte, I know you didn't get a fracture like this from falling. In order for your wrist to break at an angle that way, someone had to grab and twist your arm. Hard."

"He didn't mean to," she whispered.

"Charlotte—"

"Please don't. Please."

Her plea-filled eyes gazed at him with such intensity, such trust, there was no way he was going to push this further. But where did that leave him? He couldn't let her go back. But how could he stop her? And what about Toni? Could he really help either of them?

• • •

Squeezing in Mrs. Thomas had kept Toni scrambling to reschedule the few remaining patients and do her best to help without a lick of medical training. Brooks hadn't said much, but his stern expression said everything about how he felt.

"How's the day going?" Coming through the door, D.J. removed his hat and slapped it across his thigh.

"Busy. You?"

"Not much." His gaze drifted down the short hall and back. "Brooks still with Charlotte Thomas?"

Tori nodded. "He called you?"

This time D.J. nodded, but didn't have anything else to say. The hairs on her arm stood on end. She was right. She wanted to be wrong, but she wasn't. Charlotte Thomas was a battered wife. That was the only explanation for Brooks calling his brother, the police chief. The man's grim expression mirrored his brother's. A big part of who Toni used to be wanted to run back to the examining room where Brooks had been working on the arm and reassure the timid woman that all would be fine. But the woman Toni had become wasn't so sure of anything anymore.

The smacking sound of Brooks' footsteps filled the small waiting area. Not the normal tapping of boot heel on linoleum, but the full weight of all the anger and frustration that had to be coursing through him. For two days she'd watched his interaction with patients, his tenderness, his humor, his concern. The perfect country doctor. Handsome and smart, charming and caring, almost too good to be true.

"I have the x-rays." Large envelope in hand, Brooks came to a stop in front of his brother.

"You know that's not enough. She has to swear out a complaint."

Brooks shook his head. "I don't know whether to admire her loyalty and devotion to her husband or schedule her for a psychiatric eval for delusional tendencies."

"I can give it a try, but…" D.J. let his words hang. They all knew if black eyes and broken bones weren't enough to change her mind, words would have no impact.

"I know." Brooks tossed the x-rays onto the counter.

Walking past his brother, D.J. paused to give Brooks' shoulder a pat and kept going.

Like Brooks, Toni kept her gaze on the exam room door until D.J. disappeared inside. "I gather she's going back?"

"Yeah." The one syllable word was dripping with frustration. "She says it was an accident. That it's not what I'm thinking. Even insists that Jake's a good man, good husband." Brooks spun around to face her. "Tell me something. If someone had asked you a year ago if your husband was hurting you, what would you have said?"

"Denied it." The words came out faster and easier than she liked. But she knew it was true. "I don't think I would have seen what was happening. It was so gradual like—"

"A frog in boiling water," he finished for her.

She nodded. "I hate to think how long I would have continued pretending our married life was a fairytale."

"It's only going to get worse."

For a split moment Toni wasn't sure if he was talking about Charlotte or her. She couldn't blame him for thinking she might change her mind and go back to William. Especially now, with limited funds and a baby on the way. Watching Charlotte, it was easy for Toni to see the defeat she'd felt only a short while ago. But no matter what anyone might think, she was never going back. Now she was more certain than ever. She had to erase William from her life, no matter what.

CHAPTER FOURTEEN

"**D**id you cancel the rest of the day's appointments?" Brooks kept his gaze on the beat up old truck pulling away onto the street. D.J. assured him that he would have a talk with Jake, but for now, there wasn't anything they could do. The local anesthesia used to reduce the fracture wasn't technically affecting Charlotte's ability to drive, but D.J. insisted on taking her home. No doubt to have a little Come-to-Jesus chat with Jake. Later Officer Reed would bring him back to the squad car. "Yes. Your four o'clock wasn't happy but her mood improved when I said you'd be willing to drive by her place tomorrow on your way to the ranch."

"Thanks."

From behind the counter, the muffled sound of her cell ringing broke the awkward silence. Toni fished the phone out of her bag in the cabinet and frowned at the screen.

"Who is it?"

"Caller unknown." Swiping at the phone, Toni held it to her ear. "Hello?"

"What the hell do you think you're doing?" Even without the speaker phone on, Brooks could clearly hear the man on the other end. The unhappy man. "No one gets away with divorcing me."

Toni stiffened, and Brooks inched closer. Normally in an obviously private conversation like this, he would have slipped away into his office and allowed the couple to work their differences out. But this wasn't normal. This was Toni and her asshat of a soon to be ex-husband.

"Your mother would have a heart attack. Do you want to be the cause of your mother's death?"

"I don't think—"

"That's just it. You don't think. I do the thinking in this family. I have enough headaches with these morons on this project. You call your lawyer right this minute and tell him this was all a mistake."

Toni's grip on her cell phone tightened, her cheeks grew pale, and she momentarily rocked in place.

"If you don't, I'll make sure he never practices law in the state of Massachusetts again. Or do you want to ruin his life, too?"

Toni closed her eyes and worked her mouth open, but the asshat never gave her the chance.

"You'd better get to that lawyer and fire him before I do." Some mumbling sounded in the background. Words Brooks couldn't make out. "Damn it. I have to go. And Toni?"

Political correctness be damned. Brooks sidled up behind her, close enough to hear her staggered breath, and placed his hands on her shoulders. The slight tremble beneath his fingers had him biting down hard on his back teeth.

"Yes," she answered softly, tears building in her eyes.

"Don't fuck this up like you do everything else." On that bitter note, the line went dead and Toni dropped the phone like a hot iron.

Without a thought, Brooks spun her into the fold of his arms, and lightly kissed the top of her head, the way he would a hurting child. "It's going to be okay. I promise you the entire Farraday clan is on your side."

Her head buried in his shoulder, Toni mumbled into his shirt. "I don't know the entire clan."

"Doesn't matter. If it matters to me, it will matter to everyone in the family."

Toni pulled away, her head tilting back, her watery eyes staring up at him. "And do I matter to you?"

So many emotions swirled in the depths of the dark-blue waters staring back at him. The same torrent of emotions slowly eroding his good sense rushed inside him. Raising his fingers to rake through the blonde curls at the back of her head, his grip tightened. Holding her in place, he lowered his face, their gazes holding. "Very much," he whispered one second before his lips pressed hard against hers.

• • •

The feel of Brooks mouth on hers shocked her system like a splash of the icy Atlantic on an early summer day. The welcome sensation would ricochet through the human nervous system and, coupled with sunshine and warm sand, trigger all the happy hormones available. A simple press of lips was all that and then some.

Tender, sweet, soft, caring, and…wrong. "No," she mumbled, not totally sure if she was talking him into stopping or herself out of it.

Not that it mattered. Instantly freezing in place, his body stiffened, and his hands fell to his sides. It took another very long moment for him to take a step in retreat. "I'm sorry."

She couldn't find words to respond. The only thing kicking around in the daze of her mind was "I'm not" and that would be totally and completely uncalled for. Wouldn't it? "I…"

He took another step back and ran his palms down the side of his legs. "My Aunt Eileen would take a switch to me if she'd caught me."

"Good thing she didn't catch you." She didn't like the awkward air that hung between them. She wanted to make it right. Make it like it had been the last few days. Simple conversation amongst new friends. Only another part of her wanted him to come close and kiss her again. And again. Oh God, what was happening? She couldn't get rid of one man and run straight into the arms of another. Especially another man who seemed too good to be true. "If we're done for the day?"

He nodded.

"I think I'll walk home. Meg should be there by now."

"I can drive you."

"No. I can use the fresh air."

Brooks took another step back. "This may not be the best time to bring this up, but did you speak to your attorney today?"

"Briefly. He told me that he'd successfully arranged for the papers to be served through the consulate where William is." She walked around the reception counter and reached for her purse. "I guess we know he got them."

"Did the lawyer say what happens next?"

"Much the same as with any divorce. It depends on what William does, but I'll bet my last dollar that his next phone call was to his legal team."

"Maybe we should tell D.J. what's going on. He may want his officers to keep an extra eye out for William or his henchmen."

"William doesn't have henchmen."

"That's what Meg probably thought."

"What?"

"It had never occurred to Meg that her cheating, stealing ex would come after her here in town."

"Oh, that." Slipping her phone into her purse Toni slid the straps over her shoulder. "I guess we're both lousy judges of characters."

"Not anymore."

"No. Maybe not Meg anymore. I guess I'll see you tomorrow."

"Toni."

She turned back to look at him.

"We're not all asshats."

"No. Maybe not." With a smile and a nod, she turned and headed out the door. She'd made it less than two stores down when she spotted a pretty white and blue layette in the window of the quaint looking Sisters shop.

Stepping inside, the old-fashioned bell over the door jingled and a tall, slim woman with strawberry blonde hair scurried out from behind a floral curtain. Not more than a few seconds behind her appeared another woman short and plump with a platinum blonde nest of hair teased as tall as she was wide.

"Oh, hello. You must be Meg's friend," the taller one said. "I'm Sissy. This is Sister. How may we help you?"

Sissy and Sister? Well, the shop *was* called Sisters. "I'm just browsing. I saw the baby clothes in the window."

"Oh," the shorter woman rubbed her hands together. "We just love babies. Don't we Sissy?"

"That we do, Sister. Is our Meg expecting?"

Toni recognized the gleam in the redhead's eyes. It was very similar to her Aunt Celeste when she was about to sink her teeth into some juicy gossip. "No. I don't think babies are on the agenda until after the bed and breakfast is up and running."

"And she's doing a lovely job of it," Sister chimed in.

"You'll find all of our baby apparel over here." Sissy led the way to the far left corner. The shop was much larger on the inside than it appeared from the curb. Scanning the tables and racks, Toni realized this was much more of a general store than a boutique. She rather liked that idea. And she liked Sister and Sissy too. As a matter of fact, she liked all the people she'd met, except for Jake Thomas. Tuckers Bluff had a hint of Mayberry, but who didn't like Mayberry?

Instinctively her hand fell to her stomach. There could be worse places to raise a child.

CHAPTER FIFTEEN

rooks was still watching the Sisters' shop across the street. As soon as Toni had stepped outside, he'd moved to the window to watch. An absurd need to follow and protect her drove him to continue watching. Before her call from her husband, for obvious reasons Brooks knew he didn't like him, but hearing the man, having that personal connection, thinking of him laying a hand on Toni made Brooks' skin crawl.

From inside his pocket, his cell phone sounded off. Miami area code. "Hello."

"Hey, this is Brooklyn, getting back to you."

"Yes. Thank you. I can't tell you how much I appreciate the help."

"No problem. I owe Declan a lot more than a little background check."

Whenever talk of life in the Marines came up, former marine Declan James Farraday, brushed off the idea of danger. Brooks wasn't surprised that any of them would do that for their Aunt's sake, but he'd have expected D.J. to be more up front with his brothers. Then again, some things a man keeps to himself. War would definitely be one of them. "Find anything interesting?"

"Depends what you call interesting. As far as I can tell he doesn't cheat on his taxes, but with the amount of money this guy is sitting on, if I dig a little further I'm sure some dust will rise."

"Okay. I'm onboard with anything that puts this man away. What else?"

"Mr. Bennett seems to have a temper problem."

No shit.

"One that his mistress is none too pleased with."

"His what?"

"You heard right. He's got cajones, too. Three years ago he moved the girlfriend, Nancy Cameron, into a posh pad in the same building he lives in with his wife."

"Son of a …"

"And here's the kicker. The mistress has a restraining order on him."

"Really?" Now wasn't that interesting.

"Seems he got a little too rough a little too often."

"A little?"

"He put her in the hospital for a week."

"Shit." There was no way Brooks was letting this guy near Toni or the baby – ever.

"The interesting thing is, the timing seems to line up with the first time Mr. Wonderful turned on Toni."

"Any idea why the two-timing bastard snapped?"

"Still working on that one, too. But you and I know guys like this don't change. They only get worse. The sooner we get this character out of her life the better. In the meantime, we'll keep digging. This guy stinks. If there's anything more to be found, we'll find it. I promise you. And by the way, tell Toni we'll have a nice thick file, if she needs it, when it comes time to work out a property settlement."

"Thanks. Keep me posted."

"Will do."

So many things in this world would never make sense to him. Men like Jake Thomas and Toni's husband were at the top of the list.

Just as his stomach growled, Toni came out of the Sisters' shop swinging a small bag. If he hurried, he could catch up to her. He was going to have to share what he'd learned and they both needed to eat. According to his aunt, bad news was easier to swallow with a good meal or wash down with a decadent dessert. He knew just the place to serve both.

• • •

Less than halfway between Sisters and the corner of Meg's street, the familiar rumble of Brooks' truck slowed beside Toni. "I got some additional info on your soon to be ex. Hop in, I'll drive you the rest of the way."

After the earlier kiss, as chaste as it was, the last thing Toni needed was to sit next to Brooks. Chatting with the sisters over baby clothes and the pros and cons of disposable diapers, pacifiers, and formula, Toni's mind had drifted off to that sweetly tempting kiss. The slightest of touches that still had her feeling a little lightheaded. And it was that very lightheadedness that also convinced her that her response was nothing more than hormonal. The thing was, she wasn't interested in putting the theory to test. "A very learned source tells me exercise is good for me."

Brooks chuckled at how she'd thrown his own instructions back at her. "Your learned source is absolutely correct." While she stood in place, he pulled up against the curb, rolled up the window and climbed out of the vehicle. "I should follow the same advice." The next thing she knew Brooks had swooped the bag out of her hand and settled in step beside her. "Doesn't feel like you bought very much."

"Yarn."

"You knit?"

"No."

"But you bought yarn?" He shortened his stride to match hers.

"It was Sisters' idea."

His chin dipped in understanding. "They can be very persuasive."

"They gave me a lesson."

"Just one?"

"Sissy said it was all I'd need."

His head bobbed again, slowly, less convincing of his agreement. "So you bought the yarn?"

"It seemed like a good idea at the time."

"And what are you going to make?"

"A baby blanket. They said crocheting would be easier. One hook, hard to drop stitches."

"I think that's what my aunt does. She and the other ladies of the social club spend most of their time socializing or playing cards, but they still like doing blankets and other gifts for new moms. Sort of a town tradition."

"It's a nice tradition."

"We have a lot of them."

"Really?" Having been born and raised in suburbia, there weren't many traditions that survived the invasion of modern technology and made in China. "Like what?"

"Well, the town still does a pot luck lunch after church on the first Sunday of the month. Folks who live pretty far and don't make it into town for weekly service come on the first Sunday."

"And everyone brings a dish?"

"Yep. We've got some pretty awesome cooks and bakers in the county."

"I bet. Recipes probably passed down for generations." Some of her best recipes belonged to her grandmother.

The closer they came to the park down the hill, the more clearly a child's squeals could be heard. The way Brooks zoned in on the little kid spinning on the playground merry-go-round, he too had mistaken the fitful giggles and laughter for painful cries.

"I've been by here at least once every day and this is the first time I've seen anyone in that park."

"After school is when you're most likely to see kids playing. Sometimes a few moms will come for a play date, but it's not like it was when we were young."

"More kids then?" She'd stopped walking to watch the mother spinning her two children around on the colorful spinning wheel.

"Actually, with the population growing and more folks living in town there are probably more kids now then back then. The sad thing is they're probably parked in front of their video games or computers."

"Funny, here I feel so far removed from modern times." Instead of continuing along the sidewalk, Toni took a few steps onto the grass, still fascinated with the scene in front of her. "I keep expecting to see a Studebaker amble down the road, or teens in poodle skirts come out of the drugstore."

Brooks laughed. "The town can have that affect on people. But even Tuckers Bluff hasn't escaped the changing times. Whether we like it or not twenty-four-hour news channels and the Internet have brought the world into our backyards."

"But you still do pot luck church dinners. Barn raisings?"

He laughed again. "Not exactly."

"What exactly?"

"There's usually some sort of church bazaar to raise funds for what insurance doesn't cover."

"Told ya." She wandered deeper into the small park. "They had one of those in a nearby park when I was young, but they took it out. My mom said it was too dangerous."

"Not surprised. When I was a kid we'd spin that thing so fast until kids began flying off, one by one. The 'winner' was the last one holding on for dear life."

"Okay, when you put it that way, removing it from the playground makes sense. Though I wonder why this one is still here?"

"Maybe because parents with kids weaned on horses aren't that scared of what an old fashioned merry-go-round can do."

"I guess. I was more a swing girl. I can almost remember the rush of pushing the limits higher and higher. As a kid it was the coolest thing."

Turning to his left, Brooks pointed up at a large, old oak tree. "See that branch up there?"

There were a lot of branches. "You may want to get more specific."

"The one above the monkey bars, sticking straight out and then suddenly elbowing up."

"Yeah?"

"While the other kids were horsing around on the monkey bars during a Fourth of July picnic—"

She couldn't help but smile. The Mayberry look-alike had an annual town picnic.

"—Hank crowed how he could stand at the top of the monkey bars. Adam and I decided to show him."

"Uh oh."

"We shimmied up that tree and stood at the edge of the branch crowing like Tarzan." Despite whatever was coming next, Brooks looked up at the tree as though he were admiring an old lover. "Then we heard the first crack."

"I knew it." She tried to smother a laugh with her hand. "The only reason I'm not horrified is I know you and Adam don't appear to have any permanent scars."

Brooks pulled up his sleeve and turned his wrist. "Could have been worse. Adam broke my fall. He was on crutches for six weeks. And when we were both cast free, Dad had us doing chores for old man Brennan after we were done with ours. Something about learning to use our heads instead of landing on them."

The mother announced it was time to go home and fix supper. The two young boys grumbled under their breath and then decided it would be more fun to race to the sidewalk. As the kids flew by, the mom came to stop beside them. "Hi Doc. I swear one of these days those two are going to run out of energy." The two boys approached the sidewalk. "Wait for me." She turned back. "I'd better go. Nice seeing you."

"Don't let them wear you out too much!" Brooks chuckled at the sight of the young mother chasing down her kids. Turning back to Toni, he set his hand on her lower back and nudged her forward. "Let's check it out."

"Oh no." She eyed the now still rainbow-colored piece of playground equipment. "I am so not spinning on that thing."

"Not the merry-go-round." He took a few more steps and waved ahead at the swings. "Go for it. I've got your back."

CHAPTER SIXTEEN

The plan when he'd chased after Toni had been to take her out to the Lakehouse Restaurant. On the outskirts of Butler Springs, it was the go-to place for a night out. From everything he'd learned about her and all he was about to share, he figured she'd deserved the treat. Stopping to play like a couple of kids at the playground was the last thing he expected to be doing. Listening to her laugh as she pumped as high as she dared, he couldn't think of a better place to be.

"This is still fun," Toni called from above and then cackled with joy as she dipped past him and up the back side of the metal bars. On her next turn forward, he noticed she'd stopped pumping and waited for her to wind down to a halt. "Adulthood is so overrated," she giggled.

Extending his hand, he pulled Toni to her feet and then stood by as her legs found purchase beneath her. "Careful, Captain Jack."

"That really was fun. I don't think adults have enough fun." She took a step forward.

"My aunt would beg to differ. And from some of the card games I've watched. I'd have to say those old gals have plenty of fun."

"Maybe." At the foot of the swings, she dipped to pick up her bag from Sisters, then turned and stretched her hand out to retrieve her purse from his shoulder. "Thanks."

As much as he hated to spoil her good mood, there were things to talk about.

"I can tell you have something you want to say, so go ahead. I'm all ears."

"Am I that easy to read?"

Toni shrugged. "I've watched you a lot the last few days. There are few traits all the brothers have."

"Like?"

"Well, today with Charlotte Thomas, D.J. was your mirror image. There's a deep set between your brows that isn't strong enough for a frown but definitely shows your displeasure. But the real giveaway is your eyes. There's an intensity to them that brings to life the old cliché if looks could kill."

"If it weren't illegal I would gladly take Jake out behind the woodshed and teach him a lesson he won't soon forget."

"I believe you would."

The old oak with the elbowed branch where new growth had sprouted after the groundskeepers had sawed the end clean twenty years ago shaded two plastic picnic tables. "Shall we have a seat?"

Toni quirked a brow at him. "Bad enough to want to tell me in private?"

"I don't know." He honestly didn't know. For any normal couple he'd expect the news to be devastating. But how would an unhappy soon-to-be ex-wife feel? That he hadn't a clue.

Nodding her head, Toni eased onto the closest bench. "Okay, what is it?"

• • •

A mistress. "How long?"

"I don't know for sure. At least three years."

In her own building. Had they met? Chatted at the mailbox? Ridden in the elevator? "What does she look like?"

"I don't know." Brooks' tone was as flat as his face was expressionless. He'd said very little after dropping the bombshell about the mistress and the restraining order.

"I suppose I should get a restraining order too." If William was capable of putting that other woman in the hospital for a week for whatever infraction she'd committed, he was sure as hell capable of doing the same to her when he found out she had no intention of unfiling the divorce papers.

"That would be wise." Again his face said very little. Unlike William, who'd she'd grown accustomed to telling her how to feel and what to think, Brooks was giving her all the space and time she needed to make up her own mind.

She liked that. Liked making her own decisions again. "Yes. I think it would be. What I don't know is if I can set that in motion from Texas or if I have to wait until I go home."

This time his eyes flashed anger before an emotionless curtain descended once again. The muscles in his jaw bone twitched.

Behind his shuttered eyes she could almost see the debate, the one his grinding teeth couldn't hide. "You have something you want to say. Say it."

"It's not my place."

Not his place? "Let me see if I get this straight. You went behind my back and had William investigated, you've taken the time to inform me about his damn mistress of more than three years, but it's not your place to share what you're thinking?"

His jawline twitched again. "That's right."

"Why the hell not?" She sprang to her feet, waving her arms. It had been a very damn long time since Toni had felt even the slightest tinge of anger rising.

"I actually have quite a lot to say, but not until you've made up your mind."

"Made up my mind?" She took a step back. "What the hell about? You can't possibly be mad at me because I've never had a restraining order. Or could you?" She leaned forward. Angry enough to want to haul off and hit him. So much for a real Prince Charming. "You have no idea what it's like to slowly have every piece of you stripped away inch by inch until one day reality literally smacks you upside the head."

"I—"

"You what?" She jabbed a finger at him.

His gaze softened and for the first time since she'd met him just a short time ago, she thought she saw fear in Brooks' eyes. "I don't want to see you hurt."

Easing back onto the bench seat, Toni took in a deep breath. Maybe it was the hormones. She'd heard pregnant women were prone to mood swings. But damn it, she was in one hell of a mess and in no mood for guessing games. "I know it's probably hard for you to believe, but I used to be independent, tough, or at least I thought so." Even now, away from William, on her own again, reunited with Meg and feeling stronger, she still didn't understand what had happened. How her life had spun so far out of control. "I even had my mom's fiery Italian spirit."

"I think you just showed me some of that spirit."

His words made her smile. "I did, didn't I?"

"You were pretty mad at me that day with the dog, too. You called me mean."

Toni could feel her cheeks flushing with heat. "I'm sorry about that."

"I'm actually a nice guy." For the first time since they'd sat down, he smiled. "Even before I became a doctor everyone said so."

"I believe you." And that scared her. It was much easier if she could believe Brooks was another cardboard Prince Charming. But first things first. "Once William finds out I'm going through with the divorce plans he'll move heaven and earth to come back to Boston. I can't risk his temper. Do you think your brother can help?"

"Definitely." Brooks reached into his pocket for his phone.

Latching onto his wrist, Toni stilled his hand. "Not yet. I have to figure out a few more things. I'm afraid of what William might do if he finds out about the baby."

Brooks tensed beneath her fingertips, the muscle along his jaw pulled taught.

"After what Brooklyn reported about that woman, I've made up my mind. I'm going to have to lay low until the divorce is final." Toni sucked in a deep breath. It was probably good for her to say things aloud. "I don't ever want this child to know that monster in sheep's clothing is his father."

Until he folded his free hand over hers, she hadn't realized she was still holding onto his arm. "Normally, I would have thought there was no valid reason to hide a man's child from him."

Toni opened her mouth to speak and Brooks held up a finger.

"I said, normally. Every day, the more I learn of William, the more convinced I am that you have no other choice. Not if you want to protect your baby."

Tears welled in her eyes. "Oh, blast. Am I going to do this for another eight months?"

Brooks chuckled softly. "Probably."

"Great," Toni swiped at her eyes. "I'd better invest in waterproof maternity clothes."

"Talk to the sisters, if they don't have some, they'll know where to get them."

Just the image of the two mismatched sisters happily fluttering around the quaint shop brought a smile to Toni's face. At the same time, she found the rumbling noise in Brooks' stomach downright hilarious. "Come on. We'd better get you some food."

"That was next on my to-do list. There's a great restaurant outside of Butler Springs—"

"Another time and that would sound wonderful, but not tonight. I just want a quiet home-cooked meal."

"Of course, I understand." Brooks stood and easily his arm slid out from under hers. The evening breeze brushing over the now uncovered skin sent an unpleasant chill in every direction. There were few things she was absolutely sure of at this stage of life—but wanting to be near Brooks was a no brainer. "What would it take to convince you to stay and join Meg, Adam and me for dinner?"

Brooks stretched his hand in front of her. "I'm sure you can easily twist my arm."

Her hands barely touched his when he spun around as though his arm were contorted behind him. "I give. Dinner at the B&B tonight it is."

Helping her out of the picnic bench seat, Brooks caught her hand firmly in his. She was out of the park and halfway up the block before she even realized he was still hanging onto her hand. And damned if she didn't wish she could freeze this single moment in time, walking side by side, peaceful and happy with a man who actually gave a damn.

CHAPTER SEVENTEEN

rooks felt like a teenager walking a girl home from school. They made it to the corner of Meg's block before he realized he was still holding onto Toni's hand, and the damnedest thing was, he didn't want to let go. By the time he batted back and forth whether or not to actually let go, he was in front of Meg's house staring down at a rather unhappy Aunt Eileen.

"Let me take that for you." The decision made for him to release his grip on Toni's hand, Brooks grabbed the armload of folded fabric from his aunt.

"Those are the new parlor curtains I promised Meg." Chin held high, Aunt Eileen met him eye to eye. "You take those inside. I've got a hot dish in the truck."

"May I help with anything?" Toni's voice came out just above a whisper.

Aunt Eileen spun her gaze on Meg's friend. The fire she'd shown Brooks lingered. "That won't be necessary."

"If you're sure?"

Aunt Eileen took in Toni's meek demeanor. "I've got more curtains in the back seat. Dropped off some frozen meals for Nora. Becky and Dorothy are meeting me here. We told Meg we'd help hang the curtains and get the place looking more like a home fit for a family."

The word family had Toni's eyes momentarily circling wide before she nodded and hurried over to the truck.

Brooks moved in close to his aunt and lowered his voice. "I don't care what you think you saw. Whatever you have to say, you say it to me, later. The last thing Toni needs now is you scowling down at her. So suck it up and play nice."

Narrowed eyes that through the years had silently scolded him for anything from fussing in church to wearing his hat in the house, bore into him. The closest thing he had to a mother swallowed and opened her mouth to speak.

"Nice." He repeated. "Or go home." Retreating at Toni's nearing footsteps, Brooks turned from his aunt and smiled at Toni. "Meg is going to love these."

Already in the house, Becky and Dorothy were scurrying about the kitchen, moving dishes, pans, and enough food around to feed half the town.

"I wore my painting clothes." Aunt Eileen handed a warm pan to Meg. "Thought we'd finish up the sitting room in the master after dinner before we hang the curtains."

"Oh, that won't be necessary."

"Nonsense. The wedding is a week from Saturday. Unless you plan to have your family and friends drive back and forth to Butler Springs, we need to get cracking. Besides," Aunt Eileen smiled like the Cheshire cat, "can't have the newlywed suite feeling like a construction zone."

Meg blushed, Becky chuckled under her breath, and Toni turned away pulling silverware from a drawer. Brooks wanted to throttle his aunt for upsetting Toni. The way she silently moved, not participating in all the chatter and teasing, made him want to shove his fist in the nearest wall. Something he hadn't done since the day after he buried his mother when it finally hit him she was never coming home.

"Brooks," Aunt Eileen smiled stiffly at her nephew. "I have some more things in the truck. Could use some help."

"I'll do it." Adam, who had just come in the front door, answered.

"That's okay." Eileen patted her oldest nephew's cheek. "Brooks is already on it."

Brows raised high on his forehead, Adam looked to Brooks. There was no hiding when one of the brothers was in the doghouse with their aunt, no matter how she couched it. Maybe Brooks shouldn't have barked at her earlier and maybe holding hands with a married woman went against every rule he was raised to follow, but that still didn't give his aunt the right to pass judgment.

Ignoring the bustling people in the kitchen, Brooks followed Eileen out the front door. Marching to the truck parked at the curb, her boot heels clicked loudly against the planks of the refurbished wooden porch. As a kid, he could gauge how much trouble one of them was in by the strength of each step. Right now she could hammer nails into stone. Grown up or not, he was in big trouble.

• • •

Twenty-five years. Eileen was so spitting mad she could hear her heart pounding in her ears. Not since the day she cursed the heavens for taking her sister had she been this angry. Twenty-five years and not one of her boys had talked back to her that way. Sure at some time or another there'd been mumbling and grumbling, but Eileen had learned to pick her battles and understood selective hearing could be her best friend, but this. *Go Home,* he'd said to her. He could have slapped her with all his strength and it wouldn't have hurt as much as those cutting words. Never, not even when their mama was newly gone and the boys were riddled with pain had they mouthed back to her. Turned on her.

At the old suburban that had been hers for going on a decade, all the hurt and anger inside her had her yanking at the door with enough force to have pulled it free and tossed it across the yard. Several yards. Reaching into the backseat she grabbed the handles for the quilted pan carrier. Through the years the social club ladies had made enough of these suckers to supply every potluck dinner in the state. Right now she wanted to throw it, the truck door, and her nephew clear across town. Instead, she drew in a long breath and, lifting the warm dish of her sweet potato pie, spun on her heels to face her second-oldest nephew.

Glistening green eyes stared back at her with almost as much hurt and turmoil as she felt pulsing through her. His voice came out low and tender, more like the rumble of a well-tuned fancy car. "I love you."

Like the eye of the storm, all the fury that had swirled around her took a back seat to the quiet bond that had held this family together for twenty-five years. "Blast." The tears she'd bridled with anger pooled like a lake in the rainy season.

Taking the warm dish from her hand, in a single motion Brooks moved forward and circled her tiny frame in his massive strength. When the hell had these boys grown up?

"I'd never want to do anything to hurt you. Ever." His voice strained with the words. "But I need you to understand."

Shaking off her own feelings, Eileen looked up at the boy she'd helped raise into manhood since the age of ten. How had she missed that look? Both his father Sean and she had spotted it from nearly day one in Adam's eyes. Neither doubted that the stranger in town had won Adam's heart, even if Adam and Meg hadn't had a clue yet. And still, this was different. Eileen was torn between wanting to tan Brooks' hide for even looking at a married woman and cradling him in her arms like the boy he once was at the inevitable heartbreak a scenario like this would bring down on him.

"It's not what you're thinking." His voice was more steady, his stance straighter.

He was hurting and she hated every second of it. She may not have carried these boys in her belly, but she'd had each and every one in her heart from before their first breaths. Retreating from his embrace and sorting through the rollercoaster of emotions roiling inside her, she reached into the backseat for another bag with more drapes. "How do you know what I'm thinking?"

"Because I've thought it all myself first. And I hope you know me well enough to know I would never poach on another man's girl, let alone his wife."

Clutching the bag to her chest, she spun about and leveled her gaze with his. He was right. She did know that. Believed that about all her boys. "I do."

"Then I know it's hard, but you have to trust me."

This wasn't like the time the baseball team was suspended for having chewing tobacco in their bags and she and Sean had to choose between supporting the principal's decision and standing up for Brooks, who insisted he'd never used dip. This was wading into Ten Commandment territory. But she had to remind herself, this was the man she'd been proud of every day of his life. She sure as hell wasn't about to stop now. "I do."

A small smile graced his lips and she could see at least a little of the weight he carried lift from his shoulders. She didn't want to add to his burdens again. This situation would undoubtedly become messy enough—whatever it was.

• • •

"There is enough food here to feed an army. Who else is coming?" Adam lifted the cover from one of the trays.

At the sink, rinsing lettuce for the salad and grinning like a loon, Meg called over her shoulder to her fiancé. "No one else. What doesn't get eaten can be frozen then you won't have to worry about food poisoning when we get back from the honeymoon."

Chopping peppers and cucumbers, Toni was only half paying attention to the chatter in the kitchen. Most of her was listening for Brooks and his aunt to return. The way Brooks' aunt had looked at her as they walked up the block had her feeling about two feet tall. Not that she'd needed Aunt Eileen to tell her coming up the street hand in hand with Brooks was technically totally inappropriate, she'd figured that out for herself half way home. She'd also figured out that she didn't care, but she'd been an idiot not to think about what people would say if they'd seen them.

Walking home holding hands was a kid's move. Innocent. Innocuous. It wasn't like Aunt Eileen had caught them doing the deed in the front yard. But as bad as she felt, she might as well have. The decibel of activity in the kitchen grew as pots and pans were moved around, cabinets were opened and closed, and dishes, glasses, silverware, and napkins were pulled out. Everything needed to serve a family-style dinner. But the one sound she wanted to hear failed to occur. Why were Eileen and Brooks taking so long?

The look on Eileen's face was seared in Toni's mind. *Come on guys.* The urge to go peek through the living room curtains was almost too much to ignore. Maybe she should go outside. Explain. Apologize. Both to Aunt Eileen and Brooks.

"...would be a perfect fit."

Not until the room grew unexpectedly quiet did Toni realize Meg's last words were directed at her.

Waiting another beat, Meg set the salad bowl on the island in front of Toni. "Don't you think?"

Crap, Toni needed to answer but what the hell was the question. "I, uh."

"The house is going to be empty for a week anyhow."

Meg continued to look expectantly at her, but Toni wasn't any good at guessing games.

"I'm sorry, but—"

"No. You don't have to answer now. Just promise me you'll think about it."

Think about what?

"Sweet potato pie for dessert." Brooks crossed into the kitchen carrying a bright pink casserole dish carrier. And more importantly, he was smiling.

A few inches behind him, Aunt Eileen followed. "Not as good as those fabulous cake balls, but with Toni working all day I didn't think she'd find the time to bake too," she said. The bright grin taking over the aunt's face seemed genuine, and a strong wave of relief washed over Toni. The tension that could have been cut with a knife between Brooks and his aunt a little bit ago was almost completely gone. Taking in the room, Eileen looked around at the people waiting for an answer. "Did we miss something?"

Meg waved at Toni. "I was just sharing all the reasons staying on to help me get the B&B up and running would be a good fit for her."

Eileen held her smile but looked a bit surprised. "You're going to be staying with us?"

"I, uh," she looked to Brooks who still stood beside his aunt, but showed little expression. How she wished she could read in his eyes what he thought of the idea. It had some merit. Hadn't she only a little while ago thought Tuckers Bluff would be a nice place to raise her child? On the other hand, she'd never been fully on her own before. She'd gone from her parents' house to William's house. Did she really want to rely on anyone else ever again?

CHAPTER EIGHTEEN

"I think the most amazing thing about visiting this part of the country is the stars." On the back porch with Meg, Toni sat on the railing staring at the sky. "I don't know that I've ever seen this many stars in my life."

"I know what you mean." Meg continued rocking. "The miles of land as far as the eyes can see without even a single tree or shrub is pretty startling, and it also makes for amazing sunsets."

"I bet." *Star light, star bright; All the stars I see tonight; I wish I may, I wish I might.* "If you could have one wish, what would it be?"

"Oh, dear. I don't know." Meg kicked at the ground and rocked a little faster. "I guess, a clinic for Brooks."

"What?" Of all the possibilities, Toni hadn't expected something like that.

"Adam took over the veterinary clinic when the previous doctor retired. He got the whole operation for a song. He's done some expanding, but not much. Tuckers Bluff hasn't had a town doctor since before anyone living can remember. There's a decent clinic in Butler Springs. Anything really serious and you have to go all the way to Abilene for a major healthcare facility."

"I didn't realize."

"That's why Brooks does such good business. A lot of the folks who come in to see him come from pretty far away. For anyone living south or west of here, his office shaves over an hour drive from going all the way to the clinic."

"And he wants a clinic like Butler Springs?"

Meg shrugged. "Not sure exactly how big he wants it, but he keeps that old Suburban of his running on spit and prayer, and instead, he put his money into an x-ray machine. I could see it drove him nuts having to send patients out of town if they had a possible broken bone."

"How far is Butler Springs again?"

The screen door squeaked open and Brooks appeared. "About ninety miles the way the crow flies."

"We were just talking about the clinic." Meg smiled at her future brother-in-law.

"Adam and I finished up the last of the trim in the back bedroom—"

"You didn't have to stay so late. It could have waited."

"Not according to Aunt Eileen." Brooks flashed a sincere but tired smile. Toni was so glad whatever had passed between them hadn't proven to be a big deal, and she hoped it wasn't about her after all.

"I still say you should have gone home with the others; you have to work in the morning too."

"Sleep is over-rated." Smiling again, Brooks hefted a lazy shoulder and Toni felt the pull of the humble gesture all the way to her toes. An honest to goodness, red white and blue, nice guy. "Anyhow, before I go, thought you might want to know Adam's raiding the icebox. I think he's looking for those cake balls."

Meg shot to her feet. "They're for the rest of the week at the diner." Shaking her head, Meg hurried past him into the house, hollering at Adam. "Don't you dare."

"I love watching those two." She really did. It was like seeing a sappy movie unfolding in front of her. "Do you think they'll always be that happy?"

"Don't see why not." Brooks crossed the porch and leaned on the rail beside her. "Feel like talking?"

"What about?"

"Your next move."

"Oh." That was all she'd been thinking since Meg's offer to stay on. All through dinner, clean up, and curtain hanging, she'd kicked her options back and forth. "I hadn't meant to leave Boston yet."

Brooks nodded.

"Thought I'd have more time to save, to plan. But I already told you that."

Brooks nodded again.

"It's funny, or maybe not, how much clearer things become when you whittle them down to what really matters."

"And what really matters to you?"

"The baby. My family—Mom and Dad. I still don't want them to know about all this until it's over. As for the baby, I'll do whatever I have to in order to make sure William doesn't hurt this child."

Brooks nodded, but his expression hadn't changed. She had no idea what he was thinking.

"I already decided going back to Boston to fight this out is not in anyone's best interest. That's one point for Meg's favor."

This time, she saw a hint of a twinkle in his eyes.

"And if I don't want my family involved or at risk, that pretty much eliminates most of the state of Massachusetts and New Hampshire. So that's two points."

One corner of his mouth tilted upward toward his sparkling eyes.

"I can't imagine William trekking all the way out here, and I rather like the idea of never seeing him face to face again."

"What about the baby?"

"Yeah. Well. I'm still thinking on that one."

Brooks nodded, his face unreadable again.

"But mostly," she took a second to glance up at the moonlit night before glancing back at him, "I like it here."

"You do?" A hint of something shone in his eyes, but she couldn't quite figure it out.

She nodded. "Growing up I always thought I wanted to get away from the big in-your-face family that I had. Marrying William and into his upper-crust ways seemed the perfect answer. This town is like one huge, extended family and I realize just how much I miss that. Even the sisters. By the way, what are their real names?"

Brooks shrugged. "I don't know. They've always been Sister and Sissy."

"Oh, well. Let's just say point three in Meg's favor is I like the people here." She felt her cheeks warm with the rest of the sentence: "Some more than others."

• • •

With every word Toni uttered, Brooks' heart beat a little faster. Was this what it had been like for Adam when Meg came to town? The thought of more time with Toni had Brooks ready to kick up his heels and do a jig. All afternoon he'd been debating ways to convince Toni for her own good to stay in Tuckers Bluff where he could keep an eye on her. At least until William Bennett was fully, legally, and truly a thing of the past. Now she'd made his job a thousand times easier by coming to the same conclusion on her own, or at least the part about staying in town longer. But nowhere in his inner conversations had he anticipated being this deep down in his soul happy if she'd agree.

"Did the lawyer give you any idea how long the divorce will take?"

Toni blew out a jagged sigh. "Sort of, but not really. If William doesn't protest it could be over in a few months."

"Do you—"

Holding up her hand, she shook her head. "But from today's phone call, we both know that's not going to happen. If by some miracle he doesn't respond at all within the allotted days, the divorce can still go through quickly after that."

Now there was a possibility. "He is overseas. Maybe he won't respond. Any chance today's call was all bluster?"

There wasn't a moment's hesitation to shake her head back and forth repeatedly. "Not a snowflake's chance in Hades. William doesn't believe in empty threats."

That's what he was afraid she was going to say. "And if he

does fight you on this?"

"Worst case scenario?"

He nodded.

"Years."

Not what he wanted to hear. Maybe following up on Brooklyn's lawyer recommendations might not be a bad idea. Though a really good one was going to cost her a fortune he was pretty sure she didn't have. His mind ran through some fast calculations. He wasn't rich by any means, but money could be had. "When will you know more?"

"My lawyer said now that William has been served, how fast we hear from his lawyer will give us an idea of what kind of a fight I'm in for."

"Are you up to it?"

Toni blinked. For a second he wasn't sure she heard him. Her mouth opened then quickly closed. Then he thought she was going to nod, but instead, her shoulder lifted as though about to shrug. Finally, she closed her eyes, blew out a sigh and tightened her lips.

In half a heartbeat he'd sidled up beside her, resisting the urge to pull her into his arms, he instead tucked a loose, curly lock behind her ear. "Hey, I'm sorry."

She shook her head. "It shouldn't be that hard a question. I'd like to think so. Most of the time I'm sure I can. If not for me, for the baby…"

"But?" he coaxed.

"But he's won for so long…" Curling her fingers into fists at her sides, Toni lifted her face to meet his eyes. "I don't ever want to be a frog in hot water again."

"Don't sell yourself short. You're tougher than you think." He wished now he had his sister's gift with words. What he said next was too important to mess up. If he pushed too fast he could scare her off, but if he didn't speak up she could change her mind and leave town and he wouldn't get another chance. "Hard or easy, whatever William dishes out, you have to know you can count on all the Farradays to stand with you." Her gaze didn't falter. She didn't even blink. "And I'll be at your side to back you up or prop you up or just cheer you on. Whatever you need from me."

"So if I need someone to hold my hand?"

"I'm your man." His heart hammering against his chest, he reached out and folded her fisted hand in his.

"Or a hug?"

Tugging at her hand, he curled her into his arms. "I've been told I'm a good hugger."

"You've been told right," she mumbled into his shirt.

Wishing they'd met another time or place did no good. But holding her tightly in his arms, he was absolutely positive that no matter how long it would take for her to be free, he would be right here waiting. And if he started working on it right now, maybe she'd be as convinced as he was that here in his arms was how life was meant to be.

CHAPTER NINETEEN

"**D**oesn't the Ladies Afternoon Social Club usually play cards at the café on Saturdays?" Arms laden with trays of cake balls, Toni kicked the car door shut with her foot.

"Usually." Meg nudged her door shut with her hip. "But it would have been too much of a challenge to do the cake tasting at the Silver Spur."

That was true. The kitchen at the café was Frank Carter's territory. The guy was gruff and surly as a junkyard dog and would not appreciate her taking up even an inch of space never mind shuffling in and out with all the samples.

"I appreciate you coming all the way out here with us."

"Seeing as how you and I are the only two people who actually live in town at the moment, it only made sense for us to come this way instead of the other way around." Like everyone else in cattle country, Toni kicked the dirt off her new boots before stepping into the house. Ever since she'd agreed to stay in Tuckers Bluff for the short term, Meg and her new friends had begun transitioning her from city girl to modified country girl. The first transformation had been two pairs of blue jeans from Sisters. Becky and Meg had practically dragged her there Wednesday after work and the Sisters fluttered around laughing and fussing, pulling out pair after pair of denim jeans. Not the ludicrously expensive fashion statement she'd have found at a Boston department store, but the working kind a ranch hand would wear. The last couple of days she'd almost felt like she actually belonged in the Texas landscape.

D.J. came down the main stairs just as the two women passed by. In a smooth move, he curled his big hands on either side of the tray and slid them out of her grasp without slowing down or missing a step. "You shouldn't be carrying heavy trays."

"They're not heavy." She was all set to take them back when he winked and walking ahead, she realized he was being stubbornly protective because of the pregnancy. It shouldn't have surprised her, so far all the Farraday men she'd met seemed to be overloaded with chivalry, manners, and old-fashioned cowboy courtesies.

Only Adam, Meg, D.J. and of course Brooks, knew of her pregnancy. The rest of town, including Mr. Farraday and Aunt Eileen, thought she was staying on until her husband's time overseas was over, and to keep busy helping Meg set up for business after the honeymoon.

"How are the boots feeling?" Brooks stood toe to toe in front of her.

"You were right. These are really a great fit." She still couldn't believe that these pointy toed boots were more comfortable than her favorite walking shoes.

By yesterday Nora felt well enough to go to work. Using one of those scooter things to rest her knee on, she got around as if she were walking on two good feet, so Toni stayed home baking samples for today's cake tasting.

Brooks leaned in slightly and, for a second, she held her breath thinking he might kiss her. "How are you feeling?"

"Fine." Standing this close she couldn't seem to string two coherent words together.

He lowered his voice, "You look like you belong."

"Thank you?" She wasn't quite sure, but the way he smiled at her belonging seemed to be a good thing.

"Hey," D.J. called from across the kitchen. "Lunch break is over."

Brooks lingered a moment, and even as he backed away, his eyes remained fixed on hers until he turned and, placing his hat on his head, followed his dad and two brothers out the door.

"Where are they going?" Toni asked as casually as she could

considering how flustered a mere gaze had left her.

"They're branding and vaccinating calves. This morning they separated them from their mamas. Stopped in for lunch, and now they're heading back to the pens." Aunt Eileen was already separating the cake balls onto small plates. "How many flavors do we get to pick?"

"I think four would be good." Meg tipped her head sideways. "Don't you think?"

"I think it's brilliant to serve cake balls instead of cake."

"Well," Toni joined the ladies at the counter covered in desserts, "I'm still going to bake a cutting cake."

"Cutting cake?" Ruth Ann repeated.

"Something with a topper for the bride and groom to cut and feed each other. It's a tradition most people look forward to."

"True," Aunt Eileen said. "And it's very nice of you to agree to do all this baking."

"Absolutely," Meg spun about and flashed her friend a huge grin. "I just couldn't bring myself to send someone all the way to Butler Springs for a wedding cake and, while I know Frank's cake would have been just fine, these are going to be fabulous."

"Knock knock." Sally May Henderson crossed the room, her German shepherd, Rabb, at her side, tail wagging a mile a minute, nose twitching at the air, but steady beside his master. "Go on," she said to the eager dog. "Just stay away from the rabbits." The dog bounded past everyone and sat, tail still wagging, at the back door waiting patiently for someone to open it.

Meg stepped aside, scratched Rabb's ear and then, turning the knob, opened the door and let the eager dog out. "Look at him galloping out. Where does he go?"

"Down to the pens, checks out what's going on for a bit, then comes back."

"Really?"

Sally May nodded. "He's not a cattle dog, but he likes to think when we visit it's his job to keep the cows in their place."

"Sean says Rabb has pretty good instincts. Hard to lose that herding tendency that was bred in for so many generations."

"Sounds a bit like ranching in Texas." Aunt Eileen looked out the kitchen window in the direction the men had ridden off to. "Even now, those boys with all their own lives and careers and yet when the big jobs come along, they're back here on a Saturday working the ranch."

"Yeah. Sometimes I feel bad that Rabb doesn't have a job to keep him busy." Sally May smiled. "Other than looking out for me that is, which is why he'll be back soon."

Eileen raised her hands and eyes skyward. "And lord knows keeping you out of trouble is a full-time job for anyone."

"Hmm," Sally May ignored her friend of over twenty years, but Toni could see the smiles the two women hid. They probably knew each other's secrets and sins. Not that Toni could imagine Aunt Eileen having any sins, but still, she'd like to think if she and Meg could stay in touch this time, maybe just maybe this would be them in twenty more years.

"Okay," Aunt Eileen clapped her hands. "I've got the game set up in the big room. We can use the old buffet for all the samples so we don't have to be running back and forth."

All heads in the room nodded.

"As soon as Dorothy gets here we'll be ready to start. I've got some real strawberry lemonade on the buffet too."

"Works for me." Meg picked up two of the plates. "Which flavors are these?"

"That would be the banana with butterscotch icing and chocolate with mint icing." Toni grabbed another plate. "This one is one of my favorites, almond with white chocolate icing."

The front door swung open and Dorothy rapped on the hardwood surface. "Sorry we're late."

"No worries." Aunt Eileen grabbed a stack of paper plates and napkins. "We're just moving all the samples to the buffet."

Dorothy hung her jacket on the coat tree. "What's the plan?"

"Where's Becky?" Eileen paused looking at the door.

"She wanted to say hi to Trigger, then she's got plans with

Kelly and will be back for me later."

"Trigger?" Toni repeated.

"That's Ethan's horse," Aunt Eileen answered with a sigh.

Toni looked from Aunt Eileen to Meg, but Dorothy was the one to answer. "My Becky has been starry-eyed over Ethan since grade school."

Eileen nodded. "She's one of Grace's best friends so she spent many a weekend here growing up, but I'm afraid Ethan sees her as just another sister."

"I'd hoped," Dorothy started, "that when he signed up with the Marines, she'd forget about him and move on."

"She says that was nothing more than a schoolgirl crush," Eileen shook her head, "but she still lights up when anyone mentions his name. I've not seen her date anyone more than a few times, and if I could smack some sense into that boy of mine I would, cause they don't come much better than Becky."

"Amen," Sally May agreed, sneaking one of the orange-covered delights. "Mmm. This cake is so moist. Vanilla with a hint of... Can't put my finger on it, and the orange icing is so rich and...What's in this?"

"Oh," Toni smiled. "Each one has a different—"

"Secret ingredient," Meg cut her off. "And we'll tell you what they are after you've picked the ones you like best."

Sally May shrugged and popped the rest of the round cake into her mouth. "Sure am glad you're sticking around a bit."

"Oh my god," Dorothy held out the half-eaten, chocolate-covered morsel. "What is this?"

"Blackberry," Toni smiled. Meg had talked her into stretching her wings and experimenting with new combinations. Hesitant at first that no one would like any of them, now Toni felt really happy. With all that had gone wrong in her life in recent years even more seemed suddenly to be going right. She glanced down at her boots and could feel her cheeks pulling wider.

"What are the chances we can get that husband of yours to relocate to west Texas?" Ruth Ann reached for another sample and

Toni felt her breath catch.

Once again she looked down at yesterday's new purchase, a gift from Brooks. Turning her gaze out the window and taking in the Farraday land, she shook her head. *Over her cold, dead body.*

• • •

Brooks was simply not on his game. Not in all his years working the ranch had he been kicked by struggling calves as much as he had today.

"You're losing your touch, big brother." D.J. slapped him on the back. "There's only a couple more to go. Why don't you help Dad load the horses in the trailer? Finn and I will finish up here."

"Not a bad idea." He pulled his gloves off and shoved them in a back pocket.

"And don't piss off one of the mares and get stepped on or something."

"Hardy-har." Brooks couldn't say much more. D.J. was probably right. His head had been replaying yesterday's shopping trip with Toni. Not a good idea when dealing with a few hundred calves weighing in at over 200 pounds each. But the look on her face when they'd walked into the western supply store had stuck with him. Never had he seen eyes so bright and round in surprise. Though it made perfect sense. How many city girls get to shop someplace that keeps over fifty saddles in stock and on display along with enough western gear to outfit every cowboy in the state.

On Thursday over lunch in his office, she'd explained that Sisters didn't have much in the way of proper cowboy boots in her small size. Before he'd given it any thought, he heard himself volunteering to take her shopping at Murphy's Saddle Shop and Western Store just outside of Butler Springs. With Nora back in for a half day on Friday and his schedule already lighter than usual, there didn't seem to be a better time to go.

"All loaded up," Sean Farraday latched the trailer shut. "No thanks to you. Where's your head at today?"

Butler Springs with Toni was not the sort of answer his father would have appreciated. "There's lots going on. Sorry."

"Mmm."

Though taking his future sister-in-law's friend shopping for new boots wasn't anything Sean Farraday would take his son to task on, letting his mind wander often to how well her ass looked in those form fitting jeans most definitely was. And he had tried not to notice. A few times she'd been so adorable he'd actually forgotten she also looked sexy as hell. And considering she was buttoned up to her neck and covered to her toes, that hadn't made any damn sense either.

"What do you think?" she'd asked, looking down at a pair of sharply pointed boots that bore more resemblance to something that belonged to Santa's elf than a rancher.

"If your goal is to blend in, that may not be your best choice." Sucking on her lower lip she looked down again and Brooks had to shove his hands into his pockets and take a step back to avoid pulling her into his arms and nibbling that lower lip for her. *"Let's try these."*

She'd taken one look at the price point and shook her head.

"Humor me."

"Not a good idea."

"Please?"

Her entire face softened and showing only a hint of a smile that lit her baby blues, she huffed out a breath, sat down on the bench, and exchanged the showy wicked-witch-of-the-west boots for the butter-leather, high-end brand with a modified pointed toe pair he picked out.

"Oh, wow." She'd pushed to her feet, rocked forward and back. Then, taking a few steps forward and back, looked up at him with a full-blown smile. "These feel really good."

Arms crossed and leaning against the display case lined with every brand and design of boot imaginable in just about every color under the sun, Brooks waited another beat for her to prance up and down the aisle and convince herself they were perfect before he said anything.

When she'd come to a halt in front of him the smile had vanished. "These cost three times what some of these other boots cost." She shook her head. "I can't do that. Not now."

"My treat."

"I can't let you do that." A parallel row of creases settled between her brows just before she flopped down on the bench and tugged at a boot. "That's absurd."

"There's a reason just about everyone in these parts wears boots. Besides the fact that they stay warm in the cold and dry in the rain, they do really good in the mud and muck and the dirt and dust that blows up everywhere from Fort Worth to New Mexico."

"Doesn't matter." She yanked off the other boot. "I won't be here long enough to need all of that."

Even as she put them back on the shelf, her fingers lingered a fraction longer than necessary on the etching at the base of the medium-tan, low-heeled boots. They were perfect for her. A little artwork to reflect the northern Italian beauty, a neutral color to match her modest side, quality craftsmanship for the care she deserved, and practical for the real West Texas world.

Brooks knew he had to think fast. Very fast. Right now all he knew was he very much wanted to be the one to help put that smile back on her face. "I owe you for four days' work."

"Oh." She seemed surprised. "I was just helping."

"Yes. And I appreciate it very much. Nora appreciates that she didn't have to worry about me and my patients and she's practically singing the hallelujah chorus that, for the first time in ages, all the spreadsheets are balanced." He paused a second for that to sink in.

"Maybe." Her gaze flittered over to the boots and back.

Taking a chance, he stepped into her personal space. "If you're allowed to help, why aren't I allowed to say thank you?"

Again her gaze shifted to the boots and down to the price tag. "That has to be more than a week's salary."

Brooks shrugged. "Good help doesn't come cheap. And cheap

work—"

"Isn't good." She smiled up at him. "My father always says that."

"Then we agree? I get to buy them for you?" He could sense she was teetering but not off the fence yet. "An early birthday present?"

She chuckled, still looking at the boots.

"Christmas too?" he'd added playfully, then catching her chin with the crook of his finger, turned her to face him. "I'd very much like you to have them to remember me by."

Her eyes locked with his, so much tenderness, so much warmth. He wanted her more than he'd wanted anyone or anything in his life. Her chin dipped despite his finger still in place and not giving a rat's ass who was in the shop, who was watching, or what anyone might think or say, he lowered his head and relished in the feel of her soft, pliant lips against his.

"What, are you growing roots?" Finn had come up behind him and slapped him on the shoulder. "Whatever it is, shake it off, man. Shake it off."

"Yeah," he mumbled. No matter what went down over the next few months, there was one thing he was dead sure of: there would be no shaking off Toni. Ever.

CHAPTER TWENTY

"What the—" Sean Farraday stopped dead in his tracks and his four sons stuttered to a halt behind him.

"What's wrong?" Adam asked, his expression mirroring the concern etched on each brother's faces.

If not for the high decibel laughter filtering through to the kitchen, Brooks would have thought his father caught sight of a dead body. Or two. Maneuvering his way around, Brooks managed to squeeze into the room to get a glimpse of what his father was reacting to. The kitchen looked as though it had been in a kindergarten bake-off. Trays, mixing bowls, and a scattering of food supplies covered most of the counter and table. But the thing that had his father and brothers bug-eyed were the bottles lined up by the sink. Bourbon, Whiskey, Brandy. "Holy…"

"Eileen?" Sean called stepping over a puddle on the floor.

"In here, dear."

Dear?

Another burst of laughter from the living room exploded and Brooks and his brothers looked to their father who, slack-jawed, appeared equally befuddled by the response.

"Did you hear the one about the baker, the banker, and the bed maker?" Dorothy slapped a card on the table. "I'll take one."

"Depends on what he's making in bed," Eileen dealt the one card and smiled up at her brother-in-law. "Do you know what the secret ingredients are in," she squeaked a hiccup, "Toni's recipe?"

Sean looked back over his shoulder at the bottles lined up by the sink. "I have an idea."

From the hallway bathroom, Toni came scurrying into the room. "I'm really sorry about all this. I tried to explain that they shouldn't eat quite so many of the samples."

"Have you been eating the…" Brooks looked at the scattered plates with only a handful of cake balls remaining. "Samples?"

"Of course not." Toni Rolled her eyes at him.

"Full house, I win." Sally May laid all her cards face up on the table.

"Oh, for Lord's sake. Not yet Sally May, Meg still gets a," Eileen hiccuped again, "card."

Nibbling on her lower lip to hide a smile, Meg set her cards face down. "That's all right. I'm out."

"I'm thinking this is taking happy hour a bit far," Finn mumbled to no one in particular.

Sean spun on his heel. "I'll put on a pot of coffee."

"No need," Toni turned to the men. "I've already done that. It should be ready any minute. I tried to clean up the kitchen, but they're rather insistent I stay and play."

"My deal," Dorothy gathered the remaining cards in front of her and with a twist of her wrist sent half the deck flying. Grinning from ear to ear she shrugged. "Oops."

Scratching the back of his head, Adam surveyed the giggling women and the mess they'd made. "I thought the cakes were already made?"

Dorothy flung cards at the women around the table. "They were but I wanted Toni to show me how they're done."

"After the first batch were all gone," Toni explained, sorting her own cards.

"We really do need to get some of the lovely flavors she uses," Eileen gathered one card at a time steadily in her hand. Only the periodic hiccups gave away her inebriated state. "I really like the Mimosa balls."

"Mimosa balls?" Sean repeated.

"That would be white Chardonnay cake topped with Grand Marnier icing." Toni smiled sweetly and shrugged apologetically. "Usually the alcohol bakes out of the batter, but this time I experimented with a little extra soak after baking. I think that might be a bit much."

"Ya think?" One of the brothers mumbled from behind.

Sally May's dog lay with paws forward, ears on point, growling at the front door.

"What's up with him?" Adam inched forward carefully.

"Oh ignore him." Sally May waved a card at Adam. "He's been doing that for a couple of hours off and on since he came back from the pens. Probably a snake in the garden or a fox in the hen house."

"I keep telling you," Eileen tossed two chips into the kitty, "we don't have a hen house."

"Whatever." Sally May waved the card again and teetered dangerously on the edge of her seat.

"I'd better get that coffee poured," Sean marched into the kitchen.

"I'd say you'd better get a shower," Eileen tossed two more chips into the pot.

"I think you already anted up," Toni said softly.

"That's all right sweetie," Aunt Eileen grinned. "It's only play money. And y'all back there stink like a cow pen. Either clean up or go home and smell up your own houses."

"That reminds me," Dorothy pitched her chips center table and began singing, "There was a man named Fred, who always stayed in bed, and by and by they wondered why, they found out he was dead!"

"Oh, that's a good one!" Sally May had tears coming down her cheeks from laughing.

D.J. leaned into his brother, "What's that got to do with us smelling like cattle?"

"Beats me," Finn shrugged. "But I have a feeling this long day is about to get longer. I'll hit the showers and then take over coffee duty when I get back."

"I was going to head home and shower, but I'll wash up here in case y'all need me," D.J. added.

"What?" Finn studied him. "You don't think four grown men

are enough to handle a few tipsy women?"

D.J. looked from one brother to the other, over to the women still cackling and squealing at the table, and back to the baby of the family. "No."

• • •

Dust and dirt and miles of nothing. Why would anyone in their right mind want to spend a single day here, never mind live in West Texas?

Binoculars trained on the large ranch house windows, William followed his wife's every move. It had taken two days of travel to return to Boston from the other god-forsaken armpit of the world. Antoinette had actually thought he was still there when he'd called her. In their apartment, divorce papers in hand, it hadn't taken long to trace her location. His people were very good at finding whatever or whoever he needed or wanted.

Sleep had been irrelevant. He'd arrived in Dallas and rather than endure another flight, even a short one, he'd driven to this cartoon town in the middle of nowhere and found his wife. Working. In a doctor's office. And from what he could see, playing doctor too.

Who did she think she was fooling? Shopping for boots and hats and playing footsies with the country doctor. Betraying her husband in front of God and customers—and him. It was time to put an end to this. Antoinette belonged to him and no one else. It had taken years to mold her into the wife he needed. She was his, and he was damn well going to take her home. And just like Nancy he'd teach his wife a lesson she'd never forget. Never again would another woman betray him.

Moving closer to the house, he'd kept an eye on her and the crazy women she was with. Enough was enough. He wanted to go home and sleep in his own bed. He'd learned more than enough. Almost to the front porch he'd heard the male voices and retreated behind a tree. He wasn't worried about facing down a room full of women, but he wasn't in the mood to go toe to toe with her new boy toy.

Son of a bitch, he was ready to go home. If he was going to have to wait this out longer he would do it from the comfort of his rental car. Doubling around he heard the low rumble seconds before he spotted the furry gray animal, crouching in the distance, snarling.

Halfway between him and his car, the animal crept closer. Too far to see if it was a dog or a wolf, but close enough to know the teeth were sharp, William's choices were limited. Climb the tree, which even as a child he'd never found terribly appealing. Make a dash for the car and risk being ripped to shreds. High tail it the rest of the way to the house—and not surprisingly, facing down four grown cowboys didn't seem as distasteful as it had a few moments ago. After all, Antoinette was his wife. He had every right to take her home. Whether she liked it or not.

• • •

"Rabb, what has you all in a tizzy?" Sally May pushed away from the card table.

Staring and growling at the door earlier, now the normally friendly dog was on his feet snarling and barking and jumping at the door knob.

"For landsakes, it's just a little old snake," Sally May continued.

With a huff, Eileen pushed to her feet. "Probably that blasted mountain lion again. Only thing that can get a dog into such a tizzy is a fox or a cat."

"Mountain lion?" Toni and Meg echoed.

Toni should have realized if they were going to be out in the middle of God's country that would include all of God's creatures too. Even the ones with large fangs and nasty eating habits.

"I'll take care of it." Eileen turned a key on a large wooden cabinet and retrieved some sort of rifle.

Meg and Toni glanced at each other, no doubt thinking the same thing. This is cattle country. Having guns was no big deal. Scaring off big cats was probably no big deal either. But still…

"Better let me back you up on this." Sally May followed her friend's steps, pulled out another gun and, shifting something that made a clicking sound, grabbed Rabb by the collar. "Ruth Ann, you hang on to Rabb, please. I don't want him tangling with any big cats."

Immediately, Ruth Ann ran and grabbed the dog.

"Hurry back," Dorothy called out. "Cards are getting cold."

"Shouldn't we get Mr. Farraday?" *Or maybe just lock the doors?* Toni didn't understand why she was the only one worried about two half drunk women with loaded guns.

"Nah," Dorothy answered, "the boys are getting cleaned up. Besides, Eileen's a better shot than Sean." Dorothy leaned across the table and snatched the last Mimosa cake ball from the dish.

With the dog securely held back, side by side, Eileen and Sally May stormed onto the porch like a couple of gunslingers at the OK Corral and Toni took off running for the guest room where Brooks had gone to shower.

She hadn't realized how loud a rifle shot would be. The first one made her ears ring. The second one immediately on its heels had footsteps clamoring on the second floor. Third and fourth shots rang out and the men thundered down the stairs. Hair dripping wet and wrapped in a towel, Brooks came running up the hall.

Dorothy set down her cards and, fingers between her lips, let a loud wolf-whistle rip. Brooks came to a screeching stop and Toni nearly swallowed her tongue. Good lord did that man know how to wear a towel.

"Take that, you trespassing critter," Eileen practically cheered before firing off another shot.

"Woman, what the hell are you doing?" Sean Farraday, still in his work clothes, was the first to arrive downstairs and skidded to a halt in front of his sister-in-law. "Give me that."

"That mountain lion is back." Eileen handed off her gun and

crossed her arms.

"Where?" Pointing the gun away from the house Sean looked to the horizon.

"What the hell?" Tucking in his shirt, D.J. came up beside his father, Finn on his heels. Adam, who'd been outside in the barn checking on an animal, came racing through the house.

Another crack sounded and Sean snapped his head to Sally May, who one-handed pointed her rifle in the air. "Don't look at me, I only got off two shots. That was enough to scare away whatever had Rabb all riled up."

Sean turned back to see the dog on alert at Ruth Ann's side, his ears high, his tail still, and his teeth exposed. "You sure the mountain lion's back?"

"If you mean did I see it, no." Eileen flung her thumb over her shoulder. "But Rabb heard something. A few shots in the air would scare a bear away if we had 'em."

D.J. took the gun away from Sally May and followed his father out onto the porch. Without saying a word, Finn and Brooks turned and, each grabbing a gun from the cabinet, headed to the back. Adam snatched the gun from Brooks and looked down at his towel wrapped hips. "You'd better go put some pants on. I'll check the barn."

"Good thing y'all don't have a hen house." Dorothy was on her feet and taking one of the last blackberry cabernet balls. Toni wasn't sure if for the older woman this was just another day on the ranch, or if maybe someone should take the cake balls away from her.

"Ah jeez, Eileen." Sean lowered the gun, his eyes staring to his left. "Damn good thing you were shooting in the air. And you know what goes up comes down. Lucky it's not raining bullets on us." He pointed at a big tree not far from the house. "It's just a dog."

"A dog?" Finn muttered.

All heads turned to see Rabb still secure at Ruth Ann's side. Adam worked his way back into the house and returned his weapon safely in the cabinet. "I'd better take a look at the dog."

Sean nodded.

"We're going to have to check the rest of the trees too." D.J. pointed to a nearby fallen limb. "If those few bullets were all it took to bring down that branch, something must have rotted out the tree."

"The drought could have something to do with it."

"I thought the drought was over." Meg inched her way to the front to get a look.

"It is. But that doesn't mean there isn't plenty of damage in its wake." Adam kissed his fiancée on the cheek and eased around her. "I need to get out there. See whose dog is loose."

"You don't think…?" she asked him.

"Honey, it's been months." He kissed her on the forehead. "If I need my bag from the truck, I'll let you know."

Meg nodded and Toni moved by her friend. She wanted to see what was happening up close but was still a little shaken with all the guns going off.

"I wonder," Meg walked out to the porch and took a spot next to Eileen and Sally May.

Sticking close by, Toni came to a stop beside her college friend and looked to where everyone had been pointing. A medium sized furry animal glared at the fallen tree branch, growling.

"It's him," Toni and Meg echoed.

"Him?" D.J. turned.

"The dog," they chorused.

"You've seen that dog?" Meg asked.

Toni nodded. "The first week I was here. It was on the street."

Brooks came up behind her, placed his hands on her shoulders and looked to where Adam was slowly inching forward, cooing soft words at the snarling dog. "Yep. That's him."

"You've seen him too?" Meg looked from her friend to her future brother-in-law.

"You might say we met because of the dog."

"Really?" Meg raised a brow then returned her gaze to Adam.

"I guess you could say the same thing about Adam and me."

"Really?" Toni looked at the dog. "He was so sweet the time I saw him. Do you think he's hurt more? Could that be why he's snarling?"

Brooks squeezed her shoulders in a comforting gesture. "If he is, Adam will take care of him."

All eyes on him, Adam made it within fifteen or twenty feet when the dog gave a single bark and scurried twenty or so feet back.

"Oh no." Toni jerked forward. "He's getting away again."

"Hang on. Give Adam a chance," Brooks reassured.

Adam hunched down and called to the dog. The big fella plopped his tail on the ground and gave another bark. Slowly, Adam eased up, took a couple more steps and stopped, then taking several quick broad steps, hunched down again. Only this time instead of calling the dog, he reached forward, shook his head, and called out, "Houston, we have a problem."

CHAPTER TWENTY-ONE

The last thing Brooks expected to come across on the ranch was a dead body. Brushing his hands, he pushed to his feet. "Broken neck. Nothing anyone could do."

"Who the hell is he?" Still on his haunches, Adam looked to his brother. "And what the hell was he doing hiding behind this tree?"

With Brooks out of the way, D.J. finally got a chance to get a good look at the face. "Oh, shit."

"Oh shit what?" Adam turned to his brother. "Having a dead body in our yard isn't bad enough?"

"This is Toni's husband."

"What?" Brooks took another look at the guy. "He's supposed to be in the Middle East. You sure?"

D.J. nodded. "Yeah. Brooklyn sent me a report of everything he had on the guy, including an 8 x 10 photo. It's him." Getting up from the ground, D.J. looked up at the overhanging branches. "So you're saying death by tree limb."

"Officially the cause of death is broken neck. This isn't a typical accident. There might have to be an autopsy to confirm."

"Wait a minute." Adam stood huddled with his two brothers looking at the jagged tree limb. "Is this going to be a problem for Aunt Eileen? I mean, her gun…"

D.J. shook his head. "It's not like she was shooting at him. This is ranch country, we use our guns. Under normal conditions, a few rounds in the air to scare off an animal wouldn't have done this kind of damage. Call it a perfect storm of sorts. Limb condition, a few bullets, and this asshole needed to stand in just the right spot."

Adam looked around for any signs of the dog. "I wonder if

that was him?"

"Him?" Brooks asked.

"The dog on the road the night, or morning, I met Meg."

"That's right." D.J. looked around as well. "He seems to be good at disappearing."

"Among other things." Brooks looked down at the dead guy and his skin went cold thinking about the possibilities. Suddenly Toni's soon to be ex-husband seemed even more crazy and dangerous than Brooks had thought. Chasing her down halfway across the country. Stalking her on his family's land. And how long had he been following her? Had he ever really left the country? What would he have done with her? Too many ugly questions with even uglier answers. "We'd better move him into the barn. I'll call Andy. He can keep this guy on ice until the coroner can get him."

"We're sure the ladies are okay?" Adam asked again.

"Again with the second guessing me." D.J. glared at his brother. This had been almost a joke between them, but right now, not so much. "I'm positive. Nothing to hide here. I'd better go talk to Toni."

Brooks reached out and snatched his brother's arm. "Let me."

"She's going to have to identify him."

"I know." Brooks took in a long breath and walked back to the house. This was not something he was looking forward to.

First to greet him at the edge of the porch were his father and Finn.

"What is it?" Sean Farraday asked.

"The shots hit a rotted limb. Landed on Toni's husband. Broke his neck."

Wide-eyed, his father and brother looked like matching owl bookends.

"I'll explain later. I need to talk to her."

Inside the house Meg and Toni stood waiting for news of the mysterious dog, the other ladies were back at the table, though no card playing had resumed.

"Is the dog okay?" Toni asked.

"Probably. As soon as I got there he took off, but from what we could see, he seemed perfectly healthy."

"No limp?" both women asked.

Brooks shook his head. "No limp. But we need to talk," he said to Toni.

"Okay."

"In private. Let's take a walk out to the barn." Putting his hand along the small of her back, he directed her toward the kitchen and called out to his aunt. "Going to show Toni some of the horses." He didn't wait for her response, just kept walking.

"How far is the barn?"

"Not very. Far enough away so we don't smell the animals, but close enough to tend."

Once inside Brooks grabbed a blanket from the tack room, spread it out across a stack of hay, turning it into a bench of sorts. "Sit." He directed.

"Okay. I'm sitting. What's wrong?"

"It's William." Her brow furrowed and he sandwiched her cold hand in his. "There's been an accident." There was never an easy way to say this. "He's dead."

She gasped, and her free hand flew to her mouth. Her gaze studied his, questioning the veracity of what he'd just said, and then she let out a long breath. "What happened? Is anyone else hurt?"

Brooks shook his head. "He wasn't overseas."

The lines on her forehead deepened. "Boston?"

Brooks shook his head again and squeezed her hand. "Toni, he was here. Probably coming to take you home. The tree fell on him. Broke his neck. He died instantly."

"Are you sure?"

"That he's dead? Yes. That it's William?" He nodded. "D.J. identified him, but you'll have to confirm."

Silently she nodded and he battled around all the things he would say or do in different scenarios. None of which made sense now.

"I should be sad. Or at least feel bad." She closed her eyes. "Am I a horrible person that all I feel is relief?"

"No. You're human. William was a manipulative abuser. Relief is perfectly normal."

She opened her eyes and stared down at their hands. Seconds ticked by and she batted around another set of crazy ideas.

"I'll have to go home to arrange for the funeral."

"Does he have family?"

"Yes." Her gaze shifted down the center hall and lingered a moment. "I don't want to see them. I don't want to have to pretend to be a grieving widow."

"You don't have to pretend anything."

"I don't want to be disrespectful. It wouldn't look right if I weren't there. I never liked his mother, but still…"

She angled her head and stared blankly. He couldn't begin to fathom what she must be feeling. Her mouth opened and shut, making no sound. When she struggled for words once again, he put his finger over her lips. "This is complicated. There are a lot of years between you and William. It's okay to need time to think this through."

Toni sucked in a deep breath and then blew it out slowly.

"But when you're ready," he continued, "I'll be waiting for whatever comes next."

Her gaze softened and she squeezed his hand. "I think I'd like that. Very much."

• • •

"This is your last chance. No changing your mind again or on Saturday you'll slice into a cake from a box." The last few days had been a whirlwind of ups and downs for Toni. Happy and at peace for the first time in years, her stay in Texas had been heaven. Except for the problem with Charlotte Thomas and even that didn't seem so bad knowing D.J. had gotten involved and was now watching Jake carefully. And then Saturday came along.

"No more changes. We're going with the white cake, the chocolate, and the banana. But are you absolutely sure you want to do this, Toni? This is a small town, moving the date back wouldn't be impossible." Meg stood still, watching her friend closely.

"Nonsense." She and Meg had been carrying on this conversation for days. "Your parents and friends from out of town have made their arrangements, everyone around here has busted their butts to get this house ready for company, the tent people are scheduled to set up all the venues at the ranch, and I think if you make Eileen wait another week the woman may die from anticipation."

"You may have a point about Eileen. Adam says she's been driving all the ranch hands crazy for weeks."

"You see." Toni blew out a sigh. "I'm fine. William's mother and sister didn't question the coroner's conclusion of accidental death. Wrong place, wrong time, it happens. No one mentioned my cake balls or Aunt Eileen's gun. His family insisted on handling the arrangements, and because of the autopsy and transferring the body from out of state the funeral won't be until next week. So you see, there's nothing for me to do back in Boston, and there's no reason to postpone your wedding ceremony." Toni turned back to her baking. "Besides, you didn't even like William."

"That may be true but it seems somehow disrespectful to have a big wedding celebration on the heels of Saturday's accident." Looking out the kitchen window, Meg sucked in a deep breath. "But what I really care about is you."

Putting aside the cake mixture, Toni spun around to face her friend. "I'm not going to lie, there's a lot going on here. But right now there's nothing I'm looking forward to more than seeing you marry the man of your dreams."

"Better." Meg laughed and turned to Toni. "I dreamed of Chris Hemsworth and Zach Efron.. Adam beats them both hands down."

"That he does." Toni smiled at her friend. *And Brooks beats*

Adam and the others hands down.

"Knock knock."

Toni's heart leapt at the sound of Brook's voice. He'd been at her side helping her sort through this mess as close to 24/7 as possible without crawling into bed with her.

"All right," Brooks set the cardboard box on the counter and pulled out the first bottle. "Sister ordered extra Grand Marnier and Butterscotch Schnapps. Apparently Sissy loved the orange and Sister is fond of the banana and butterscotch and they want to make sure there's enough to last the entire party."

"And probably leftovers for a doggy bag." Oven mitts in hand, Toni pulled a fresh pan from the double ovens. "I really do love this kitchen."

"Good." Meg picked up her to-do list from the opposite counter and hugged it to her chest. "Because now you have no excuse not to stay and help me get this place off on the right foot. Even the left foot would be better than instant oatmeal and frozen waffles."

"You can do better than that and you know it."

"Maybe," Meg grinned, moving toward the doorway, "But now we won't have to find out. I've got a few calls to make. When Adam gets here, let him know I'm in my office."

"Will do."

Brooks took the last bottle of liqueur the sisters had ordered for Toni out of the box. "How much more work do you have to do?"

"Just one more cake batch has to go into the oven and then I can call it a night."

With his back to the wall, Brooks leaned against the cabinet and crossed his ankles. "I could watch you cook all day."

"Oh, that sounds exciting." Toni poured the batter into the greased pan.

"You're looking good." He eased away from the counter. "You're amazing."

"It's just cake balls."

"That's not what I meant." Crossing the expanse in a few steps, he pulled the oven door open for her. "You've been through so much and yet here you are chugging along like any other day. I keep expecting you to fall apart any minute. To need me here to catch you. Hold you up. But nothing. You're stronger than you look, Toni."

Only a week ago, having Brooks standing this close to her would have had her all out of sorts. Fogged her brain and sent her heart racing. "There were a couple of days this week I wasn't so sure."

Brooks waited for her to shut the oven, then sidled up beside her. "You're not still blaming yourself?"

Her head bobbed, moving from one side to the other, not quite a nod, not quite a shake, not even somewhere in the middle. "Every day I wake up and think there must have been something I could have done differently. That somehow this is my fault. If I hadn't filed for divorce. Hadn't been a coward and waited to leave him till he was away. Just one thing done differently maybe—"

"Toni—"

"No. Let me finish. Once I go through the blame game that he's dead then I grab my mind and remind myself that none of this was ever about me. No woman could have made him happy. Normal. Not even his mistress."

Brooks winced. Toni was pretty sure the idea of William cheating on her bothered Brooks more than it did her, but understanding that William could easily have put Toni instead of his girlfriend in the hospital was a sobering jolt of reality for both of them.

Lightly, he ran the back of his knuckle down her forearm. "Any man would be proud and honored to have you as his wife."

Those words and the gentlest of touches, combined with the intensity of his gaze as he trained his eyes on her, sent Toni's heart galloping at full speed. After all she'd been through, all the promises she'd made to herself about never trusting another man again, how could one man make her love again so hard and so soon? "Oh my God."

"What?" Concern washed over his face, his other hand rose to encircle her in his strength. Not to control, but to protect, to care for, to…

"I love you." The words tumbled out, sounding just as surprising to her ears as they had when she'd realized them moments ago. She wasn't infatuated, in lust, or even falling in love. She loved this man deep down to the tips of her toes. The way she'd never loved anyone ever before, and wasn't this one hell of a way to tell him, standing in the kitchen covered in flour and surrounded by wedding cake balls.

Surprise opened his eyes wide, and then slowly his face relaxed as his gaze bore into hers, studying, examining, searching for the truth. She knew he found it when the corners of his mouth tilted up very slightly. "I guess that's a good thing because I fell for you the second you told that stray dog I was a *mean, big man*."

That made her laugh. For the first time in days, she felt light, truly light. Until his mouth came down on hers, and this time there was a hunger she'd never felt from him before. A passion that had been kept at bay and was now safe to unleash and, dear Lord, how her heart pounded and her head spun. She couldn't pull him close enough, for the first time she felt the moist warmth of the tip of his tongue begging for admittance and she wanted to crawl inside him.

The oven buzzer sounded and she couldn't care less. Long fingers laced through her hair and held her to him. The hand on her hip kneaded and swirled adding to the heat rising inside her.

Footsteps pounded in the distance, and Toni didn't stop. Kissing this man for the rest of her life seemed like the best plan she'd ever had. And if this was a dream, she didn't want it to end.

The buzzer stopped and a deep male voice rumbled from a distance, "What the hell?"

In her mind, Toni recognized Adam's voice, and still she didn't care.

"I was just thinking that myself," Meg said from nearby, the most likely reason the blaring sounds of the obnoxious oven timer no longer filled the room.

Sliding his hand away from her hair and down her side, Brooks rested it on her other hip and slowly pulled back just far enough for his lips to barely touch hers. Close enough for his breath to continue to fan the flames sizzling inside her. Close enough for only her to hear. "I love you, Toni."

Adam cleared his throat, and Meg's footsteps moved away from this side of the kitchen and toward her fiancé. "Let's go, handsome."

"But.."

"Not now, dear. They've got a lot to work out if Toni and I are going to become sisters."

"But…"

"Look at it this way," Meg's voice faded as they walked out of the room. "Once she gets used to the idea, Aunt Eileen is going to be thrilled with only five single Farradays to go."

EPILOGUE

"**G**ood heavens, man. It's a neck tie not a noose." Adam shoved his finger in his collar and yanked at the knot Connor had tightened.

"Maybe if you did your own tie…" Connor let the words hang.

"I'll fix it." Brooks stepped up to the eldest Farraday son and adjusted the tie that went with the new shirt and dark suit.

Two raps sounded on the door. "Ready or not, I'm coming in." Grace, the baby of the family, popped her head into the groom's ready room. "You gentlemen all set? The guests will be arriving any minute, Aunt Eileen is pacing the halls like a caged lion, and Meg is probably the first bride in the history of mankind to be ready ahead of time. Let's get this show on the road."

"Send a gal to law school and she comes home a tyrant." Connor loved having a couple of days with the entire Farraday clan. Even Ethan had wrangled leave for the wedding.

Shaking her head and rolling her eyes, despite the fancy updo and the makeup and the curvy figure, all Connor saw was a feisty tween exasperated with her older brothers. "All I know is the ushers better be downstairs before that first guest arrives or I won't be held responsible for whatever Aunt Eileen does." Flashing one very bright and toothy grin, Grace backed out of the room pulling the door shut.

"You certainly don't need all of us to tie your tie." D.J. adjusted the knot on his own tie and reached for the doorknob.

"I'll come with you." Finn followed his brother. "The two of us should be able to keep Aunt Eileen from a coronary."

"It's going to take a lot more than one little wedding to get Aunt Eileen out of sorts." Connor shook his head and followed on

Finn's heels. "But just in case ..."

The four younger Farraday sons gathered in the church vestibule. "So tell me," Connor leaned into the only brother still on active duty with the military. "Was it bribery or blackmail that got you a pass stateside?"

"Neither. The timing was just right." Almost as an afterthought, Ethan flashed a grin most likely meant to reassure, but all it did was worry Connor more. He'd been in the marines long enough to know coincidences like this rarely happened. Something was up with Ethan and the hairs on the back of Connor's neck told him whatever it was the Farradays might never find out, even at the foot of a flag-draped coffin.

"Hey, what has you two looking like your dad caught us TPing the Rankin house?" Becky Wilson slipped out from the small room off the side of the church where Meg and the other bridesmaids were ready and waiting to walk down the aisle. Her gaze stuck on Ethan. "Uniform looks good on you." Her grin was huge and Adam was right, her eyes still lit up like a kid with a favorite toy when she looked at Ethan.

Connor shifted his attention to his brother decked out in Marine dress blues. The guy may be a brilliant pilot, but he was an idiot when it came to Becky. Any man would kill to have a girl look at him with that kind of adoration. Especially one as sweet as Becky.

"Heads up. Here we go." Ethan clicked his heels and moved to the massive oak doors, extending his elbow to Sally May. The floodgates were now open. As if a pistol had been fired announcing the beginning of the festivities, the townspeople flowed into the church dispersing equally on both sides of the edifice, friends of both bride and groom.

By the time the brothers lined up at the front of the church with the old organ striking the chords that sent all guests to their feet, Connor was actually feeling almost as nervous as Adam. Except the man who couldn't tie his own tie thirty minutes ago now stood at the front of the altar beaming like a lighthouse bulb on a New England coast. Not a lick of nerves could be seen, the guy's gaze pinned to the beauty in a flowing, white dress gave Connor gooseflesh.

Beside Adam, Brooks, the best man, the guy in charge of the all-important rings, the one who should have been swatting bullets from the responsibility, was tracking Toni up the aisle in front of Meg. A couple of months and two brothers down for the count. And the bastards looked the happiest Connor had ever seen them. No doubt he'd be back in town very soon for another Farraday wedding. Though under the circumstances, he suspected it might be a tad smaller. But then again, what did he know. Other than he'd willingly slay dragons, fight giants, and face down a wild beast with his bare hands if it brought him the right woman.

Enjoy an excerpt from

Connor

"**M**y heavens, Ralph." Still holding onto the doorknob of the upstairs bedroom, Eileen Farraday took a step back. "When was the last time you were in this room?"

Ralph Brennan, the Farraday ranch neighbor for longer than Eileen had been with the family, came to a stop beside her. "I guess a while."

"A while?" She looked over her shoulder at him. She'd walked the second floor halls of the well-kept ranch house for the first time since Marjorie Brennan passed years ago. Everything looked exactly the same, including Marjorie's sewing room and the stack of pink fabrics she'd used to make Grace's third birthday party dress. Sucking in a breath and forging forward, Eileen surveyed the remaining rooms upstairs. Dusted and clean, Marjorie would have been proud of him. Time had stood still in the Brennan house.

"I figure it's time."

Eileen's brow arched high on her forehead and out of respect for the nearly ninety-year-old man, she refrained from blurting out the first words that had come to mind, *Ya think*?

"I told Catherine I would be with her soon, but I needed to get this old house in order first. Don't want no strangers pawing through Marjorie's things."

It took Eileen a few long seconds to remember who Catherine was – the Brennan granddaughter. Eileen had never met the child, but when Ralph's wife had passed from a long bout with cancer, the little girl had been many a topic of conversation at the Farraday kitchen table. "You're going to see your granddaughter?"

The old man's smile lifted. "Yep. She's an important lawyer where she lives in Chicago. Too hard to come to Tuckers Bluff, but I told her as soon as I get things straightened out here, I'll be heading her way for a visit."

Eileen looked down the hall. If he wanted to visit his granddaughter before the next millennium, Eileen was going to have to call in some backup. "I'll need help."

Ralph Brennan squinted. "What kind of help?"

"Extra hands. Or you won't be seeing Catherine for a long time."

"Already seen her." The man grinned at Eileen again.

"When did you leave town?" Maybe the old goat wasn't as sharp as everyone thought.

"Ain't left the ranch. Saw her on that contraption she sent me."

Contraption?

Ralph turned and walked down the stairs. Eileen figured she'd seen enough upstairs and fell into step behind him.

At the bottom of the stairs, he made a sharp right into what she knew to be his office. The room probably held records for a good fifty years or more of Brennan Ranch business—all in handwritten logs. "This thing."

Eileen chuckled, relieved the old guy wasn't losing his mind. "A computer tablet."

Ralph shrugged, then flashed a toothless grin. "She's pretty as a picture. Looks just like her mama when she smiles." He hit a switch and a photograph of what Eileen assumed was the granddaughter, now fully grown and with a young child, appeared on the screen.

"She's lovely. Hope she makes it out this way some day."

"Don't know about that. I've been waiting almost a year for that to happen and finally gave up. That's when we agreed these old bones would have to go north if we're going to visit. It's better that way for Stacey."

"The little girl?"

"Her little girl. Cute as a button." A quick frown descended over his eyes.

"What's wrong?" Eileen tread carefully. Ralph wasn't one for talking, so she knew the only way to find out what had his mood turning was to ask and then hope she hadn't stepped on any toes.

"Not sure. Little girl doesn't smile and doesn't talk. Catherine says she's just shy around new people."

"Lots of kids are that way."

"Maybe." He huffed out a ragged breath rubbed his hands together. "I wasn't too keen on leaving, but now that it's been decided, I'm rather anxious to get going. When can you get started?"

"I suppose the easiest place to start is with Marjorie's sewing room. There are lots of folks in town who could use those supplies. Maybe we'll start doing up the quilt tradition again."

"Marjorie always enjoyed making those baby quilts. Nothing made her happier than being with children. Always thought it a waste she wasn't mama to a dozen little ones, but guess the good lord thought one was enough. And late in life at that."

Eileen smiled at him. "I'm sure there were times we'd have been happy to lend you one of the boys. Or two."

"You done good with the boys. Made them right men. It does my heart good knowing this place will someday be raising Farraday children again."

"Again?"

"My great grandpappy bought this land from the first Farraday. His wife didn't like living so far away from everything. She was from some place up north, Boston maybe. Anyhow, she had a hard time adapting to the ways of a rancher, but the isolation was the hardest for her. Fearful she was going to lose her mind, he sold this land to my kin on the condition that the house be built close to the property line. That way the ladies were able to visit back and forth. Worked out just fine as both women were city girls."

"I didn't know that story." Eileen wondered how many more things the old coot had tucked away in the corners of his memory that he'd never shared. "Not much more to tell. Farradays and Brennans been neighbors ever since."

"No hidden feuds?" Eileen teased.

"Nah," Ralph shifted his weight. "Not even a bicker. My sister Edna almost ran off with Sean's Uncle George. That was fodder for the town busybodies for years. Edna was only fourteen and she and George had run off to the justice of the peace all the way in Butler Springs."

"Really?" Eileen would have to ask Sean if he knew the story. Otherwise, she knew what the topic of conversation would be at the next big Farraday reunion.

"Foolish young kids. Two years later Edna married one of the Turner boys and moved to Butler Springs. Eventually, your Uncle George met his Martha and moved to her neck of the woods. That's about all the excitement there ever was."

"Well, it sounds fun. So," Eileen clapped her hands, "why don't you find something to do, and I'll get started upstairs."

"If you don't mind, it's past my afternoon nap time. I think I'll just have a seat here and watch a little TV. Maria left a fresh pitcher of lemonade in the fridge."

"Why don't you take a seat and I'll bring us both a glass."

Ralph smiled at her. "You're a good woman, Eileen. You done right by your sister, and now you're doing right by my Marjorie."

"That's what neighbors are for, Ralph." It wasn't often anymore that the memory of her sister's life cut short so young still stung hard. Something about being in this home where time seemed to have stood still made the hurt fresher than it had been in decades. Eileen continued into the outdated kitchen. While the Farraday kitchen had been redone just before she'd arrived on the ranch, the Brennan kitchen looked like the set of a seventies sitcom. Harvest gold was the color of choice. The only sign of the modern world was the stainless steel microwave tucked away in the corner. Even the refrigerator was an ancient pull handle model, a throwback to an even earlier decade. Eileen couldn't believe the dang thing still worked. Though on second thought, it shouldn't surprise her. The fridge came from the days when appliances were built to last a lifetime, or in this case, several lifetimes. Two chilled glasses in hand, Eileen returned to the large den. "Here you go, Ralph."

His eyes closed and lips curled upward in a smile, she didn't see any reason to disturb his pleasant dream. Setting the glass down on the table beside him, an odd sensation skittered up her spine. Her heart took off in double time and she took a closer look at the peaceful smile. "Ralph," she whispered, slowly reaching for his arm. Eileen pressed two fingers on the inside of his wrist.

Closing her eyes tightly, she moved those same fingers to his neck. "Oh, Ralph."

MEET CHRIS

USA TODAY Bestselling Author of more than a dozen contemporary novels, including the award winning *Champagne Sisterhood*, Chris Keniston lives in suburban Dallas with her husband, two human children, and two canine children. Though she loves her puppies equally, she admits being especially attached to her German Shepherd rescue. After all, even dogs deserve a happily ever after.

More on Chris and her books can be found at
www.chriskeniston.com

Follow Chris on Facebook at ChrisKenistonAuthor
or on Twitter @ckenistonauthor

Questions? Comments?
I would love to hear from you.
You can reach me at chris@chriskeniston.com

Made in the USA
San Bernardino, CA
28 July 2017